Mystery surrou

And that constantly
More than anything
met him under diffe...

"Is it difficult for you to accept things that don't lend themselves to explanation?"

She nodded. "It's a combination of private skepticism and police training. I'm more comfortable with hard facts."

"Then rely on this—you can trust me. No matter what goes down, I'll be right there with you. You'll never have a better partner."

"Or a more dangerous one," she muttered.

Somehow, he managed to hear her. "Dangerous to others perhaps, but never to you."

Even as he spoke, he could feel her responding to him. What was drawing them together was nature at its most basic…and more. No woman had ever gotten under his skin like this, making him ache and wish for things he had no business wanting.

Dear Reader,

Writing is remarkable work. It fulfills an author's spirit in a way very few things can. That's not to say that everything during the course of a book flows smoothly.

While working on *Navajo Courage,* I spent lots of time hiding out in my office. Somewhere along the way, I'd forgotten that ideas come from life itself.

Once I realized my mistake, I immediately shut my office door and went to join my husband and our animals. By the end of that day, inspiration had dawned and the story came together.

I learned then that the barriers we put around ourselves all too often lock us in and keep us from getting what we most need. Using that newfound knowledge, my hero, Luca Nakai, and the heroine, Valerie Jonas, quickly blossomed to life.

People tend to think of writers as loners, shut away somewhere. But the truth is that's not the way it works. People need people. It's that simple—and that complicated.

Here at Harlequin, for example, I'm part of something much bigger than just my book. Since 1989, Harlequin Intrigue has been home for my work—and for me. It's a place filled with the support an author needs to create stories from the heart. Everyone bands together to bring you the best stories possible. In the process, a real sense of family unfolds.

I'm proud to call myself a Harlequin Intrigue author. Happy 25th anniversary, Harlequin Intrigue, and thank you very much for allowing me to be a part of your history.

All the best,

Aimée Thurlo

AIMÉE THURLO

NAVAJO COURAGE

HARLEQUIN®

TORONTO • NEW YORK • LONDON
AMSTERDAM • PARIS • SYDNEY • HAMBURG
STOCKHOLM • ATHENS • TOKYO • MILAN • MADRID
PRAGUE • WARSAW • BUDAPEST • AUCKLAND

To my sister Silvia, and my other sister Peggy.
Love you guys.

Recycling programs
for this product may
not exist in your area.

ISBN-13: 978-0-373-69421-1

NAVAJO COURAGE

ABOUT THE AUTHOR

Aimée Thurlo is a nationally known bestselling author. She's a winner of the Career Achievement Award from *Romantic Times BOOKreviews,* a New Mexico Book Award in contemporary fiction, and a Willa Cather Award in the same category. She has been published in twenty countries worldwide.

She also cowrites the bestselling Ella Clah mainstream mystery series praised in the *New York Times* Book Review.

Aimée was born in Havana, Cuba, and lives with her husband of thirty-nine years in Corrales, New Mexico. Her husband, David, was raised on the Navajo Indian Reservation.

Books by Aimée Thurlo

CAST OF CHARACTERS

Tribal Police Detective Luca Nakai—As the son of a medicine man, he was eager to do battle with his tribe's ancient enemy. But his attraction to the beautiful city detective was an unexpected—and dangerous—complication.

Sheriff's Detective Valerie Jonas—The hard, street-smart cynic didn't believe in Navajo magic—not until she met Luca Nakai. Together, they stood a chance… but just barely.

Stephen Browning—A former reporter with a serious lack of ethics, he'd do anything to break the biggest story in years.

Professor George Becenti—He took pride in his Navajo blood and thought he knew everything there was to know about Navajo witchcraft. Was he Browning's secret source, or Valerie's worst nightmare?

Frank Willie—He quit school abruptly, then his girlfriend moved out. Now the woman was dead, and he was running from the police, desperate to protect his secrets.

Dr. Finley—Head of the anthropology department, the maverick professor knew how to stir up trouble. What's worse, he liked being the center of controversy.

Mae Nez—Her best friend had been one of the first to die. Now the skinwalker had her in his sights.

Deez—Mystery clung to the Navajo elder like second skin. Yet seeing through the web of secrets surrounding him could help the hunted become the hunters once again.

"I bring disturbing news, Cougar," he said, using Luca's code name. "Word has reached us that a murder that carries the signature of a skinwalker has been reported outside Albuquerque," he added in a barely audible voice, his hand reaching up to grasp the flint arrowhead he wore on a leather strap around his neck.

Luca understood *Diné Nééz*'s caution. To speak the word "skinwalker" out loud was said to call that evil onto you. Speech was more powerful than the Anglo world realized…or would believe.

"*Bijishii* suggested that you have a Blackening done before you go," he said, referring to a well-practiced rite. Blackening cloaked an individual against evil. The rite would give him the power of Monster Slayer, who'd defeated all the evils that had preyed on The People at the beginning. "He'll also be preparing a special *jish*, medicine bundle, to help you."

Skinwalkers…. Navajo witches. They hid under the skin of a coyote or a wolf while they roamed the night spilling blood. Deluded or not, these men or women were feared—and with reason.

"Is this a Brotherhood assignment?"

"It is. The skinwalker has issued a challenge to us. The sign of the Brotherhood of Warriors, flames bounded by a circle, was left in ashes near the body. The officer who first responded is one of us, and sent word to me immediately."

Now, at long last, he knew why he'd been chosen. As the son of a *hataalii*, Luca had knowledge that would give him the only power obtainable over this enemy.

"The Brotherhood will be close by if you need backup. The code word that'll allow you to recognize another warrior is *hasih*. The counter is *bideelni*."

Appropriate. The greeting, loosely translated, meant "hope." The answer meant "to make it happen."

"Understood."

Luca brushed aside the heavy wool blanket covering the entrance to the hogan and went inside. The interior had been warmed by the burning piñon logs in the central fire pit. He sat on the ground on the south side and faced his father, who was seated on the west side behind the small fire.

Diné Nééz followed him in and took a seat beside Luca.

After a momentary, preparatory silence, *Bijishii*'s voice rose in a chant that vibrated with power and echoed with tradition. The richness of his voice sparked the air as the animal-hide rattle punctuated each sound.

When his song ended, *Bijishii* looked at his son. "The cougar is your spiritual brother and that connection will strengthen and prepare you for what lies ahead. Like cougar, you've become a master hunter, but for this assignment you'll need to draw on cougar's other attributes—his strength of will, intuition and steadfastness."

Luca watched as his father assembled the contents of the new medicine bundle he'd be carrying. The *jish* would be tailor-made to fight the dangers he'd be facing on this assignment.

"Flint will repel the *chindi,* the evil in a man that survives death but remains earthbound," *Bijishii* said. "Flint's power comes from its hardness and the flashes of light it emits. It represents lightning, and the moments just before dawn. I'm also placing a piece of turquoise in the bag. That'll honor Sun, who placed Turquoise Man inside his own child to make him invincible. There's corn pollen in the *jish,* too. That'll feed the spirit of the cougar," he added, then held out his hand. "Hand me your fetish now."

Luca gave his father the small stone carving he carried with him in a special pouch.

"Everything inside this new *jish* will keep your spiritual brother strong. Call on him, and he *will* help you defeat your enemies," *Bijishii* said.

Bijishii burned five herbs in a fireclay container. He then placed a spear point–shaped flint within the ashes. As the Blackening began, *Bijishii*'s song recounted how the Holy People had taught the Earth People to use Blackening as a protection from evil.

As his father's voice rose in the confines of the hogan, Luca could feel the raw power of the ancient rite strengthening his spirit. In the days ahead, he would be challenged repeatedly and his life might even hang in the balance. But he was a member of the Brotherhood of Warriors and a tribal police officer. This was his destiny.

Chapter One

It was nearly 9:00 a.m. on a muggy August morning and Detective Valerie Jonas of the County Sheriff's Department wasn't in a good mood. She'd just received a cell phone call from her watch commander.

Another body had turned up less than a half hour ago, yet here she was at the Albuquerque Sunport. The chartered flight from Shiprock delivering the special investigator from the Navajo Police had been delayed—naturally.

Right now she should have been at the crime scene, working, not cooling her heels. It was true that the first murder, and the second from what she'd been told, held the stamp of tribal magic. Yet she'd need to focus on forensic evidence, not superstition, to solve the crimes.

Valerie adjusted her badge, making sure it showed as clearly as the pancake holster at her belt. The procedures for an officer at this airport were clear. Although none of them could fly armed without filling out a boatload of paperwork, they were able to carry a weapon throughout the airport terminal and facilities.

On her way to the gate—a long walk to the small local carrier's location—Valerie answered two more calls from the Sheriff's Office. The days of handheld radios were gone, and most detectives now lived with cell phones attached to their ears.

At the far west end of the terminal, Valerie noticed a Pueblo

Indian man, small of stature but with ample girth, looking around with apprehension as he accompanied another man into a hallway off the main corridor.

She slowed her step, her instinct for trouble working overtime. As she passed the small corridor lined with snack machines, she glanced down it. The big, no-neck blond in a knit shirt and dark blue blazer was standing nose to nose with the Pueblo man, pushing him against the wall. The muscular Anglo also had something in his hand—a weapon maybe. Unfortunately, from her vantage point, she couldn't swear he wasn't holding a cell phone.

She moved to the side of the crowd hurrying past her, stopped and watched out of the corner of her eye. As she looked on, the Pueblo man reached into his pocket, brought out his wallet and handed it over to no-neck.

Her body tensed as she realized what was going down. The goon was probably armed with a pointed weapon of some sort, perhaps something made of hard plastic that could pass through the electronic screeners.

As the robber glanced around quickly, Valerie turned her body so that her service weapon wouldn't show and avoided eye contact. If the robber identified her as law enforcement, he might panic and turn his victim into a hostage.

Somehow, she had to get closer. Then she'd make her move. Reaching into her pants pocket, she brought out a handful of coins. Then, jiggling the loose change in her hand, she drifted toward the vending machines as if contemplating a snack.

She was easing down the corridor when a tall, good-looking Navajo man brushed past her.

"Excuse me, ma'am," he said, giving her a cocky half grin that was so intensely masculine, it practically took her breath away. His gaze still on her, he collided hard with no-neck, knocking him to one side.

Catching a glimpse of the semi-auto in no-neck's hand, Valerie instantly reached for her weapon but, in a heartbeat, the good-natured Navajo man underwent a transformation.

Positioned just right, and with no wasted motion, he moved in like a Special Forces pro. Brushing away no-neck's pistol with his left hand, he stepped up and decked the robber with a bone-jarring punch to the jaw. To Valerie's surprise, the pistol fell to the tile floor with a rattle instead of a thud.

"The gun's a toy, Officer. Check out the vic." The Navajo man flipped the groggy thief onto his belly, then produced a set of handcuffs from beneath his jacket and quickly secured his prisoner.

Valerie called for backup as she went to help the victim, who'd just taken a puff from his asthma inhaler. Verifying that he was all right, she went to join the Navajo man whom she now guessed was either undercover security or a police officer.

As she drew closer to him, she got her first clear look at the Navajo fighter. Her earlier impression had been incomplete. There was far more to him than just a charming smile. His eyes were a deep brown and burned with fire and determination. Broad shouldered and strong, but not muscle-bound like the blond hugging the ceramic tile, he had the kind of masculinity that reached out to a woman with a whisper, not a shout.

Glancing up at her, he met her gaze and there Valerie saw an inner stillness, a quiet confidence that added a whole new dimension to the strength and ability she'd already seen him display.

With effort, Valerie brought her thoughts back to the business at hand. Fantasies were for vacation and off-duty hours. "You knew the perp's gun wasn't real. That's why you weren't concerned about taking direct action. But *how* did you know that?"

"No oil or gunpowder scent," he answered.

She blinked. In a terminal filled with fast food, perfumes and aftershaves, it would have taken a bloodhound to pick out oil or gunpowder residue. He had to be kidding.

"Do you have an evidence bag?" he asked, going over to where the weapon lay.

"Yeah, I've got several—just not handy," she said, then, hoping she was right and this was her new partner, added,

"I'm Valerie Jonas of the Sheriff's Department. By any chance are you Detective Luca Nakai of the Tribal Police?"

"That's me," he answered. Though the terminal was loud and people were starting to gather, his low, sexy voice carried clearly.

Pen in hand, he bent down and retrieved the realistic-looking toy by the trigger guard. "This guy might need an EMT to check him out. He went down pretty hard."

The robber moaned and, suddenly realizing he'd been cuffed, kicked out at Valerie.

She tried to dodge, but stumbled from the glancing blow to her calf and fell against Luca. He was built solid and the hard expanse of his chest was like iron and steel, but that warmth…

Luca steadied her, then moving away, caught no-neck scrambling to his feet and swept his legs out from under him with a well-placed boot.

The handcuffed man fell to a sitting position, then realizing he was outmatched said, "No more, I'll stay still," and scooted to put his back to the wall.

Two armed airport security officers joined them seconds later. Valerie turned the prisoner over to them, gave a quick rundown of the events then pointed out the initial victim, who'd kept his distance.

"We're needed at a crime scene right now, guys, but here's where you can reach me," Valerie said, giving the closest man her card. Luca handed the toy gun to one of the officers.

A short time later, Luca walked downstairs with Valerie, heading to the terminal's east end where the luggage carousels were located. On the way, he watched her as she used her cell phone to report the incident to a Captain Harris.

After a few minutes, the attractive detective closed up the cell phone and glanced at him. "Sorry about that. Right after I arrived at the Sunport to pick you up we got a call. Another body has been found apparently with the same M.O. as the first one. Deputies are on the scene now."

He didn't comment, waiting for her to fill in the rest when she was ready. Detective Jonas—Valerie—was beautiful…electric almost. Light auburn hair fell over her shoulders and her gray-green eyes sparkled with intelligence and purpose. He noted that there was no ring on her finger, nor was there the impression of one that had been recently removed.

As they walked down the terminal she answered two more calls. From the way she focused and shot questions at whoever was on the other end, he suspected he'd been paired with a woman on a mission, and maybe with something to prove. Not his type, despite her obvious intelligence and physical appeal.

Yet as he gazed at her, he was aware of an unexpected stirring in his blood, and recognized the familiar tug in his gut. He'd felt neither in a very long time, not since…

Valerie answered one more call, speaking quickly to whoever was on the other end.

With the rush of people, conversations going on all around him and the thud of luggage as it slid off the conveyer belts on the carousels they passed, the quiet of the reservation seemed like a distant memory. His new partner's never-ending conversations grated on him as well. She was *definitely* not his type. Not that it mattered. He was here to do a job then return home—hopefully in one piece.

They stopped by the last luggage carousel, which had already stopped rotating. Only eight passengers had come in on the small craft so finding the right piece was easy.

Luca slid his hand around the handle of the canvas duffel bag he'd brought and, as he lifted it off the turntable, noticed the way she was looking at him. Awareness clawed at him. Cursing chemistry and hormones, a bad combination that could only lead to trouble, he clamped a lid on distractions.

"Did I forget to say thanks?" she asked, interrupting his thoughts. "You came up with some pretty good moves back there."

"Thanks," he answered simply, then followed her up the stairs and out of the terminal.

Soon they were on a wide sidewalk, a north-facing loading

and unloading zone. He turned to the west and followed, coming up beside her.

"Not exactly the talkative type, are ya?" she asked after a brief silence. "Well, that's okay. I'll do enough for both of us, Partner."

"I've noticed."

She laughed. "I wouldn't want you to get bored," Valerie said as she led the way past the shuttle vans. "Not that there's much of a chance of that, not on this case," she added, growing somber as she got back to the business at hand. "The body found this morning was in the city, not county, but since the M.O. matches, it's my case, too. The county crime scene unit is already there. City detectives will no doubt be there as well, standing by and looking over my shoulder every step of the way."

"Do you happen to have the full report detailing the first crime scene?"

She nodded. "It's on the seat of the car. You can study it on our way to the number two site."

He didn't respond.

"Did you hear me?" she added.

"Of course."

"Then grunt or something, will ya?"

He paused, then added by way of an explanation, "Conversation… There's more of a demand for it out here in the city."

They soon reached a white unmarked sedan with local government license plates. While she unlocked the door, he noted the folder on the passenger's seat.

"How much do you know about the last killing?" she asked as they both got in.

"I was briefed by my captain. I know that the murder suggested a Native American connection—Navajo, to be specific."

"Yeah. The cause of death was the result of stab wounds from a large knife. What made it—shall we say unusual?—was that the victim was also stabbed with a blade shaped from a human thighbone. The M.E. was able to narrow that down via fragments recovered from the wounds. Pieces broke off when the bone blade hit the victim's ribs. There was a lot of weird symbolism at the scene, too. You can see that in the photos."

He nodded, studying the folder's contents.

"My first thought was that it was some sort of Satanic or Goth ritual, but one of our officers insisted that it was connected to Navajo witchcraft. He said that the powder we found scattered on the body, what he called corpse poison, was a trademark of skinwalkers. The M.E. confirmed later that it contained human tissue. We also found coyote hairs on the victim's skin and clothing. Locks of her hair had been cut off, probably with the murder weapon. One last thing—interesting, not to mention weird—the tips of both index fingers, actually the entire joints, were cut from the body. They weren't at the scene, so the perp must have taken them with him."

He nodded, understanding more than he was willing to talk about yet. "Was vic number two mutilated in the same way?"

Valerie nodded. "That's what I was told, but we'll be able to see for ourselves soon enough."

As he studied the crime-scene photos, Luca recognized the symbol of the Brotherhood of Warriors that had been made from ashes and left next to the body.

"If the perp's intent had been to slow down identification of the victim, he would have taken *all* the fingertips," she said. "So the whole thing is just plain weird."

"Was either victim Navajo or part Navajo?"

"The first one's name is Ernestine Ramirez and she's Hispanic. The latest victim is a twenty-year-old woman named Lea Begay."

"The most recent victim has a Navajo name," he said. "But from now on, vic one and two will suffice."

Valerie winced. "Sorry. I was told not to use the names of the victims around you, but I forgot. It has something to do with the evil side of a person that sticks around 'cause they can't enter Heaven, right?"

"Not quite right, but you've got the idea," he answered.

"What else struck you about the first scene? Does anything in particular stay in your mind?"

"There was a small arrow with a bead at the end. It had been shot or jabbed into the victim. It was less than six inches long, doll-sized. I asked, but was told you'd explain that part."

"Arrows like those are shot from a small ceremonial bow made from a human shinbone," he answered.

"Here's something else I'd like to know," she said after a thoughtful pause. "Why were you, in particular, sent to help us with this case?"

"I'm a police detective, and more important, the son of a respected medicine man." Luca lowered his voice before uttering the next phrase. "Skinwalkers are my father's natural enemies—and mine."

"Are you a medicine man, too?" Valerie asked in a whisper, not really understanding his need for secrecy but mirroring his tone nevertheless.

He shook his head. "I trained for it but in the end I chose police work."

"The job gets in your blood, doesn't it?" Her voice was still soft. "It starts as something you do and ends up being part of everything you are."

Her observation said a great deal about her. Valerie was turning out to be an interestingly complex woman as well as beautiful.

"To catch a killer I need to put myself in his head—to see things as he does," she continued. "I hope you can help me do that. I need to start thinking like a skinwalker."

He touched the special medicine pouch he wore looped through his belt. "Don't use that word so freely," he said at last.

"Because I might call evil to us, like when I use the names of the victims?"

He nodded and said, "It's even more so with the evil ones. The spoken word has a great deal of power." He glanced down at the file. "I'm going to need a few more moments to study this file."

"No problem. We're still about ten minutes from the second site. It's past the university, near Central Avenue."

As silence stretched out between them in the car, she kept her eyes on traffic but her focus was on him. There was something magnetic about Luca Nakai—an intensity that wove its way around her and sparked her imagination. Police officer…medicine man… He was a man of many layers and something told her that beneath that imperturbable calm was a man worth getting to know much better.

Chapter Two

They were still underway and despite their silence, or maybe because of it, her attention had remained riveted on the man sitting next to her.

"You have questions about me," Luca said, still looking down at the contents of the folder.

She almost choked. Maybe he should have added mind reader to his list of qualifications. Recovering quickly, she glanced at him casually.

"You have questions about me, too, I would imagine," she said, turning it around on him. "You're a guest of our department, so why don't you take your shot first, then I'll take mine."

"You know why I'm on this case. Why were you chosen?" he asked without hesitation.

"Fair question," she said with a nod. "I was chosen because I've been given special training to deal with violent crimes against women. I've only been working homicide for six months, but I've closed all the cases I've worked on so far." Her car radio came on and she answered.

"Our ETA's less than five minutes," she responded to the caller, then, racking the microphone, glanced over at him and continued. "One big problem with this case is that we already have reporters breathing down our necks. Information about the killer's unusual signature reached the media and that's made this a hot story. The public's pushing for quick answers."

"Uncovering hidden truths often takes time. Accuracy and speed are enemies," he said, expelling his breath in a soft hiss.

"These days stories unfold quickly," Valerie answered with a shrug. "Internet and television are always in competition to see who breaks the story first."

"That's *their* problem. It shouldn't become ours. Life isn't a television quiz show."

"Off the record?" She glanced at him, saw him nod, then continued. "The problem becomes ours when the sheriff is running for reelection."

He nodded once. "I hear you. Any suspects yet?"

"No, not even a good lead. But I'll find answers. Count on it."

It was her tone that revealed more than her words. "You have something to prove on this case," he observed.

Valerie swallowed back her annoyance. If it had been anyone else, she would have told him to stuff it. Yet there'd been no censure or disapproval in Luca's tone. He'd simply stated his opinion. Knowing that he had to get to know her— after all, their lives might depend on each other—she decided to cut him some slack.

"I've had to work very hard to establish myself in my department," she answered after a brief pause. "When I first signed up, the deputy at the desk tried to talk me out of it. I'm smaller and lighter than most of the other officers. From day one, all I kept hearing was that I'd be a liability, and that I'd cost another officer his or her life someday."

He nodded but didn't speak.

"During training, I was forced to fight twice as hard as any other recruit. Nobody thought I'd make it, even when my physical training scores were better than some," she said. "Since those days, I've worked my way up the ranks to detective, but it hasn't been easy. A lot of people back from my rookie days would still like to see me fail, just so I'd prove them right."

"Why was becoming an officer so important to you?"

"Because I know I can make a difference in my job," she said in a firm voice. "My methods may be different than some of the textbook procedures, but I *can* get results."

"Different how?" he asked.

"Let me give you an example. Last week at the downtown office, a suspect slipped off his handcuffs at the booking desk and jumped the arresting deputy. He knocked the officer to the floor and grabbed his weapon. I was coming around the corner just then and, not seeing my weapon beneath my jacket, he motioned me over. I think he wanted a helpless woman hostage. I went over to him as meekly as possible. Then before he could see it coming, I grabbed the weapon and kneed him in the groin," she said. "I used the fact that I'm not threatening—the very thing they said was my biggest liability—to do what had to be done."

Luca gave her a huge, devastatingly masculine grin. "Way to go."

As she looked into his eyes and saw the approval and admiration there, her heart began to hammer. Telling herself it was low blood sugar, Valerie focused. "In this game it's all about winning, and you do that when you put the bad guys away."

"Winning… I wouldn't put it that way exactly. To me, it's more about restoring harmony—for others and within yourself."

"Inner peace? That sounds very '60s," she said with a hesitant smile, then added, "I'm not sure that kind of thing really applies to police work."

"It does. Try keeping your sanity after years of busting bad guys without it."

She kept her eyes on the road as she thought about what he'd said. Luca sure wasn't like anyone else she'd ever met. There was a quiet dignity about him and a strength that didn't rely on machismo to back it up.

"Okay, we're here," Valerie said at long last, driving down a shabby-looking neighborhood just south of Central Avenue. The street had been cordoned off at both ends of the block by APD police barriers. As Valerie held up her badge a city officer in his dark blue uniform motioned them through.

Valerie parked beside another Sheriff's Department vehicle just outside the yellow tape that defined the crime scene. The perimeter included an unoccupied-looking, flat-roofed house and a section of the alley.

It was midmorning and there were two television cameras and at least a hundred curious onlookers lining the outside of the tape. As she climbed out of the vehicle, Valerie glanced over at Luca. He was clipping his service pistol to the right side of his belt, next to his badge and a small leather pouch. Coming around the front of the car a few seconds later, he fell into step beside her as they walked toward the crime scene.

"Crazies can be real proud of their handiwork, and sometimes stick around to see us work the scene. Keep a sharp eye out for anyone who fits the profile," she said.

"Don't concentrate too much on profiles just yet. Keep an open mind," he said, then in a whisper-thin voice added, "Patience."

It was the way he'd said that word that teased her imagination, making her think of steamy summer nights someplace far away and exotic…. She shook her head, banishing the thought as quickly as it had come.

"Detective Jonas," a tall, ruddy-faced officer called out as he jogged up to meet them. "The body's through that alley at the other end, inside a private property and not visible from the outside of the yard unless you look over the wall," he said. Then, lowering his voice, he added, "the entire hood is pretty restless at the moment, so watch yourself in case a relative or friend of the victim shows up. Things could explode in a hurry."

She knew this type of neighborhood well. The residents were mostly Hispanic and Native American—people who often believed that you were either one of them or an outsider. It wouldn't make their investigation easy.

"A deputy is tracking down her family, right?"

The officer nodded. "Her residence is in the North Valley, and an officer is en route. She apparently lives with her parents."

"Anything else on the dead woman?" Valerie asked.

"She's got a student ID card from the university and crime scene found a paycheck from an area print shop in her purse. The amount suggested a part-time job. Deputy Gonzales is following up on that lead, hoping to backtrack her recent activities," the officer replied.

"Call the campus police and get her class schedule," Valerie ordered, increasing her stride.

To their left there were several old multistory apartment buildings that took up several blocks. Ahead of them, on their side of the street, were run-down single-family homes a decade or so older than the apartment structures. The fronts of the homes were open to the street, and several of the houses had low cinder-block walls in the rear.

"From what I recall, a lot of Navajo families live in this neighborhood, but I don't see any among the onlookers," she said, glancing at the crowd that lined the yellow tape cutting across the alley at both ends of the property.

"We avoid the dead. Contact with them doesn't bring anything good."

Valerie and Luca followed the tall deputy through an open wooden gate at the midpoint of the block wall and found themselves in a small backyard—the crime scene. The body hadn't been covered yet, but its location close to the wall blocked it from the view of the onlookers.

Her attention already on the body, which rested not five feet from the wall, Valerie reached into her pocket. "We'll need gloves," she said, handing him a pair.

"I'll need a second pair," he answered.

"Why?"

"Tribal officers prefer to wear two. That way we don't inadvertently touch anything that came into direct contact with the body."

Valerie called another officer over and soon Luca had his second pair. As they approached the body she glanced back at him. His focus had shifted from the body itself, and the fact that the fingertip joints were missing, to the bare earth and the items left around the victim.

"Let me know when you get the results on the green powder placed on her lips," Luca said. "I think it comes from plants used in our rituals but I'd like to know which ones specifically. You'll also want to get those strips tested," he said, pointing next to the body. "Find out if that's buckskin. Navajo witches are said to wear masks of that material at a kill site."

In a smoothed-over area of dirt by the body he could see the black outline of the circle and flames—the Brotherhood's emblem.

She followed his gaze, then pointed across the alley to the property opposite them. The wall there was covered with gang signs painted in a multitude of colors. "I saw that same symbol, or one close to it, at the first scene. Is it graffiti, spray painted onto the ground?"

"That's not paint. Take a closer look. It's finely powdered ash," he said. It had been left there as an insult to the Brotherhood. "Make sure the team takes a sample and identifies the source. It may help us in the long run."

"I'll take care of that," a young woman from the medical investigator's office answered, overhearing them. "We're ready to transport, Detective Jonas. The team leader says we've got enough photos. All we need now is your okay."

Valerie glanced at Luca, who nodded. "Go ahead," she told her. "What about the vic's belongings?" Valerie asked. "Do you have a list of what she had on her?"

One of the crime scene techs looked up then. "Her purse, with billfold, driver's license and university ID. There were some bus tokens, too. Deputy Gonzales is running down the print-shop check now. We didn't find any car keys, but there's a book bag. Inside are pencils and a pen, notebooks and an anthropology textbook."

"Let's have a look," Luca said. "Students sometimes doodle on their notes or slip papers into their textbooks for safekeeping."

"She took English lit—here's something on *Beowulf*," Valerie said moments later. "Here's another section with some anthropology notes. It's all pretty general so it must be a beginning survey class. Yeah, here it is, Anthro 101."

Luca, thumbing through the anthropology text, nodded. "This book fits that description. Any mention of a professor or TA?"

"Not yet. Wait—here's some scribbling next to some sketches of arrowheads. It says, and I quote, 'Dr. Finley sucks.' That could be one of her professors."

"Interesting wording—respecting the title but not the man—but it gives us a name to check on. Maybe Dr. Finley, whoever he is in the anthropology department, will recognize her photograph and provide us with some information we can use," Luca added. "There's a strong cultural connection to the way she was killed."

"Sounds like a plan. When we leave here, we'll go straight to the university. It's not too far back down Central, on the north side of the street."

As the body, now in a sealed plastic bag, was placed on a gurney, she studied the faces in the crowd. Their expressions told the story—along with horror and disgust there was also morbid fascination.

Praising the members of the crime-scene team who were busy placing numbered cards near each piece of evidence, she studied the camera-laden reporters. They were all struggling from behind the yellow tape for the best angles.

"Who found the body?" Valerie asked an APD sergeant working crowd control, aware that city officers were the first to arrive on the scene.

"A couple of area residents." He called her attention to two women who were seated on the back steps of a neighboring home. Another APD officer was standing beside them. "The young redhead with the short skirt and low-cut blouse was on her way home from work, and the other's a widow who was out looking for her cat. Apparently it was the cat that led both of them to the body."

Valerie turned to speak to Luca, but to her surprise saw that he'd left the taped area. He was now climbing a large elm tree to the left of the crime scene with the grace and agility of a mountain lion.

Hearing comments from curious onlookers and wondering what he was up to, she went to meet him. "What on earth are you doing?"

"The scene was carefully arranged, and I wanted to get another perspective," he said, inching out on a low limb then staring down.

A moment later he came back down. "Don't act surprised or alarmed, but someone's been watching me from the flat roof of that two-story apartment building at the east end of the block. Binoculars and gray, hooded sweatshirt—even in this heat," Luca said.

Valerie scanned off into the distance, but failed to spot the person Luca had seen.

"He's working hard to keep his face hidden. Otherwise he would have come in closer like those other folks." He gestured toward the onlookers by pursing his lips, Navajo-style. "I'm going to find out why I've got his interest."

Luca and Valerie walked slowly toward the house as if searching for something on the ground. They soon stepped into the shadow cast by the roof of the next building and there were hidden from the person with the binoculars.

In the blink of an eye Luca took off around the side of the house. He crossed the street and circled around the opposite side of the apartment building, planning to catch the guy with binoculars from behind.

Valerie shot after Luca, trying her best to keep up, though he ran like the wind. Unable to close the gap, she worked hard to at least keep him in sight.

Then, as she turned the corner, she saw their suspect climbing up the fire escape onto another pueblo-style rooftop, Luca directly behind him. A heartbeat later, both of them disappeared from view.

Knowing that Luca was on his tail, she pressed on and climbed up after them. As she reached the top of the ladder she heard a loud scraping noise somewhere ahead. Valerie crossed the roof in a crouch. Peering over the edge, she saw Luca on the parapet of the next building, dangling from one of the *cañales*. Separating Valerie from him was a fifteen-foot gap. He'd obviously jumped but had come out a foot short.

Before she could call out, he quickly pulled himself up over the ledge and onto the roof. "He's some kind of athlete, that one," Luca yelled, seeing her. "I'm in good shape, but I barely made it."

"Where did he go?" she asked, looking past Luca toward the east.

Luca studied the expanse of roof beyond. There were several chimneys as well as heating and cooling units big enough to hide behind. A moment later he looked back at Valerie and gave her a quick thumbs-up.

Valerie studied the area carefully, but all she could see were three pigeons on the graveled roof. There were no shadows anywhere to give the suspect away.

Luca pointed to the pigeons, to his eyes then to a spot across the rooftop.

It took her a moment but Valerie suddenly realized what he was telling her. The pigeons were watching the suspect.

As Luca ran across the roof a shadowy figure slipped out from behind a large chimney then dropped over the far side, apparently finding a ladder.

"Go back down, circle around and cut him off," Luca called, not looking back.

Seconds mattered. Instead of climbing back down the ladder, she shimmied down a drainpipe, dropping the last four feet to the ground and landing in a crouch.

The narrow alley was in deep shadow and constricted to one lane by two large trash bins. Hearing a footstep ahead she reached for her sidearm and, putting her back to the brick wall, moved forward cautiously.

Standing at the corner, Valerie stopped to listen. Someone took a breath. She had him now.

Chapter Three

Ducking down, gun ready, she took a quick look around the corner—and found herself staring directly into Luca's face.

She lowered her weapon immediately. "Sorry. I thought I had him."

Luca holstered his own weapon and glanced back the way he'd come. "I shouldn't have lost him, but between his familiarity with the area and his speed, he had the advantage."

"What made you spot the guy?" she asked. "There was quite a crowd back there."

"I was looking for anyone who might be paying attention to me—not the crime scene. That's when I saw him."

"I don't get it. Why focus on you? You mean because you're Navajo?"

"Not just that. I figured that a skinwalker would be watching for anyone who might be a *hataalii,* a medicine man, and wearing a medicine bundle," he said, pointing to his *jish.* It wasn't a lie, but it wasn't the complete truth either. The skinwalker, or skinwalker wannabe, had issued a clear challenge to the Brotherhood of Warriors and would have undoubtedly been looking to see who'd come in response to that.

"Did you get a close enough look to be able to make an ID?" she asked him.

He shook his head. "Just general size and shape, and the

fact that he moved like a man, not a woman. I'm not talking about fitness, just gait, okay?"

She gave him a wry smile. "No harm, no foul. I get you. But that puts us at a dead end. Let's go back and interview the witnesses."

"They may be reluctant to talk to us, particularly in a case where witchcraft's involved. Navajos aren't the only ones taught to avoid things of that nature."

Valerie gave him a surprised look. "I have no idea how you investigate a case like this on the reservation," she said, "but, out here, they can either talk or find themselves down at the station. I don't take 'no' for an answer—not when I'm investigating a homicide."

As they approached the crime scene Valerie was aware of everything about her new partner. Their styles of working were vastly different, yet she had a feeling about him. A quiet man of strength, Luca had come prepared to solve the case. She could feel his determination and understood that feeling well. They'd mesh well as partners…if only she could stop letting the fire in his eyes distract her.

Focusing back on the case, Valerie spoke to the city officer who'd kept the witnesses separated. Elderly Mrs. Santiago had been escorted home so Valerie approached the younger woman who'd remained behind. Mary Sanchez had listed her employment as entertainer, but the short skirt, revealing tank top and hard look despite her age left little doubt what kind of entertaining she did.

"I'm tired, guys, and ready to go home. Tell me what you need so I can get out of here," she said in a weary voice.

"We'll make this as quick as possible. Just tell us what you saw," Valerie said.

"It was around eight. I was on my way home—I usually cut through this alley—when I heard Mrs. Santiago looking for that blasted cat of hers. The thing's a nuisance, but it's all she's got so I decided to help her find him. I know he likes digging through the garbage, so I looked in the alley near her trash can. He was up on that wall," she said and pointed, indicating the spot just above where they'd found the body. "The cat was making such a racket I thought he was hurt, so I went over to pick him up. That's when I saw the dead girl," she said and shuddered. "I've seen people cut up before, but this was bad—real bad."

Valerie gave her time to pull herself together. A crime scene like this one was enough to rattle even a seasoned veteran.

"The blood—it was everywhere—and that Satanic stuff, right out of a horror flick. That's going to give me nightmares for the rest of my life," she whispered. "And poor Mrs. Santiago. She came up behind me for a look before I could warn her away. She nearly fainted."

"Did you notice anyone else around—maybe someone wearing a gray sweatshirt, hood over their head?" Luca asked.

"Not today. Sometimes I see people in sweats out jogging, but that's usually closer to the university," Mary answered.

Leaving her to sign the statement she'd given earlier to the county officer in charge of the crime scene team, they followed up on Mrs. Santiago.

The sergeant who'd secured the scene directed them to a house two doors down. "That woman's got to be in her eighties and she was looking downright frail. I let her go back to her home and left an APD officer with her."

When Luca and Valerie arrived at the house they were greeted by brightly colored flowers that edged the path to the front door. Although the paint on the trim was faded and the screen door looked worn, they could see that the owner had done her best with her limited budget.

Mrs. Santiago was a small woman with intelligent eyes that, at the moment, mirrored only a barely contained panic despite the presence of the burly city cop standing beside the window.

Not wanting to traumatize the elderly woman any further, Valerie released the APD officer, then, seeing a knitting basket across the room, smiled. Her mother had been an avid knitter and if Mrs. Santiago was anything like her, the activity would immediately relax her.

"Let me move that closer to you," Valerie said, picking up the basket. "That's a lovely sweater," she added, looking at the partial work lying on the top.

"It's for my niece. I'm hoping she'll come for Christmas…."

"That'll be a wonderful present," Valerie said. "I'm sure she'll love it."

Mrs. Santiago fingered the yarn absently then picked up her needles and began to knit. "I'm going to have to stop letting Oscar out. These days, between the gangs and the drugs, no one's safe. But the way that poor woman was massacred, and those things around the body…" Mrs. Santiago shuddered and her knitting needles began to click together at a furious pace. "That's not drug related or the work of the gangs around here. That's *brujería*."

"Excuse me?" Valerie asked.

"I know witchcraft when I see it—but that's not Spanish *brujería*. That's from your people, isn't it?" she asked, looking at Luca.

"What makes you say that?" he asked.

"I overheard two officers talking," Mrs. Santiago said in a hushed tone and crossed herself. "When you're old like me, people don't notice, or maybe don't care that you're there. Sometimes that's a good thing, other times it's not." She paused and lapsed into a long, thoughtful silence.

Getting impatient, Valerie started to press her, but Luca shook his head and signaled her to wait.

"Like that strange man I saw this morning," Mrs. Santiago added at long last. "He hovered around at the edges of the crowd, watching the officers instead of trying to get a look at the body like the rest of the people there. I think he was more interested in the officers' reactions than anything else."

"What was he wearing?" Valerie asked immediately.

"A gray sweatshirt with a hood. He was probably a jogger

trying to lose weight. He must have been sweating like crazy in that outfit."

"Did you happen to get a look at his face?" Luca asked. "Was he Anglo, Indian, maybe black?"

"I didn't get a close enough look. All I really noticed was the sweatshirt 'cause it struck me as odd in this heat. Then a deputy asked me a question. By the time I glanced back, the man was gone."

"How tall was he?" Luca asked. He'd never seen the person standing still up close, and it was harder to estimate the height of someone who was running.

"He was about your size and weight. But that's all I can tell you. My eyes…they don't work too good at a distance."

Despite that, their oldest witness had noticed more than most others had today. "We'll need you to sign a statement, then we'll be out of your way," Valerie said.

"Good, because it's time for me to get Oscar's lunch ready. He gets crabby when he doesn't get his tuna on time."

Soon they left Mrs. Santiago's, and, as they walked back to the scene, Valerie matched Luca's strides. He was built for strength and endurance…. The possibilities sparked her imagination.

Almost instantly, Valerie pushed those thoughts firmly back, shaking her head.

Noticing it, he glanced at her. "Something wrong?"

Just with my brain. She scrambled for a way to cover for her lapse, and then answered. "You and I need a way to communicate out in the field," she said. "We got separated back there while pursuing the suspect and things could have gotten out of hand in a hurry. Let me give you my cell phone number in case that happens again and we need to find each other fast."

As she gave him her number, he wrote it down on a notepad he'd taken out of his jacket pocket.

Bringing out her PDA, she waited for him to reciprocate but he didn't volunteer the information. After a moment she added, "I need yours, too."

"I don't have a cell phone. They don't work well enough on the Rez to make them of any real use to us. We have radios in our department vehicles and carry handhelds."

Valerie just stared at him. "No cell phone?" Had he told her that he'd just beamed down from an alien spacecraft, he couldn't have surprised her more. Her cell phone was permanently attached to her ear. She'd almost worn it into the shower a few times.

"In that case, I need to get one for you," she said after a beat. "How about a handheld radio?"

"I'll find both—a radio and cell phone for you," she said, heading over to get the emergency spares in the crime scene vehicle.

After making sure he had one of each, Valerie arranged to get the surveillance tapes from the nearby businesses, especially those within a four-block stretch along Central Avenue. Maybe they'd get lucky and locate an image of Hooded Guy.

They continued to work the crime scene until midafternoon, viewing surveillance feeds from the various businesses by using the equipment in the crime scene van. Unfortunately, none of the cameras had revealed the passage of a man in a hooded sweatshirt. He had either not been wearing the sweatshirt when passing within camera range or had traveled along a side street.

Once the crime scene unit finished with their on-site work and began packing up, Valerie and Luca headed back to her unmarked unit.

"Do you know where you're staying, or were you supposed to make arrangements once you got here?" Valerie asked him.

"I figured I'd track down a motel after I got here. Any suggestions?"

She paused, considering her answer. There was an empty furnished apartment next door to hers. She knew that her landlord would happily allow an officer to use it, too. Yet something told her that having nothing but a thin wall between them would make for some very long, restless nights. "Let me think about it while we go over to the university. We need to pay Professor Finley a visit."

Chapter Four

Ten minutes later Valerie parked her department vehicle in the empty police parking space just a hundred or so feet from the anthropology administration office. While en route they'd called ahead and learned that Dr. Maurice Finley was chairman of the department and "somewhere" on campus. He'd be sent a text message to meet them at his office.

Luca stepped out of the passenger side, admiring the tall pine trees around the older pueblo-inspired structures of the UNM campus. Large expanses of grass and plenty of shade were a welcome relief from the places in the city he'd already been to today.

Valerie reached into her pocket, feeling for the photograph of the victim the crime scene tech had printed out for them back at the crime lab van. Somehow, she doubted that it would do them much good here today. Introductory classes like the low-numbered 100 courses tended to be very large at the university, where the enrollment exceeded 26,000 students. But they had to try.

"There are probably more students here than in the Navajo Nation's largest town," Luca said, mirroring her thoughts. "Unless the victim sat in the front row of the class, chances are the professor won't have any idea who she was."

"Probably so." As Luca and she walked together, Valerie grew aware of the outdoorsy scent that clung to him. It fit him perfectly. There was something about Luca that reminded her of the rugged New Mexican desert. He belonged out in nature—just as much as she belonged in the city.

As they entered the air-conditioned building, she felt in her element. A few minutes later they were seated on comfortable padded chairs along a glass-paneled wall in the department's main office. Several people came in, including an energetic dark-haired man who glanced at them with interest after noting their weapons. The older student, probably in his late twenties and carrying a briefcase, turned to the attractive dark-haired office assistant.

"Hey, Steve," the young woman said, looking up at him and giving him a big smile. "What brings you by here?"

"I couldn't find Dr. Becenti," he said, "but the sign on his office door says he's supposed to be there."

The woman checked something on her computer monitor, then looked up and shrugged. "You're right. It's his office time according to his schedule. Maybe he dropped in earlier, but took off when nobody showed up. Did you have an appointment?"

"I didn't think I needed one."

"There's an Anasazi dig going on up in Rio Rancho. He might have gone there to check it out. You could try there next."

"Okay, Bernie, I'll give that a shot," Steve said, then left in a hurry after glancing at his watch.

A few minutes later, a fit-looking man in his late thirties, wearing slacks, a lightweight tan blazer and carrying a leather briefcase in his free hand, rushed into the office. A bicycle helmet was under his arm.

"You must be the police officers," he said, spotting them instantly. "I'm Maurice Finley." He nodded to Luca and shook Valerie's hand.

"Sheriff's Office. I'm Detective Jonas. This is…my partner," she said, unsure about using Luca's full name out loud.

Giving her an imperceptible nod, Luca answered, "Navajo Tribal Detective Nakai."

"The text message from my secretary said you wanted to

speak to me concerning one of my students. Is he, or she, in some kind of trouble?"

"Can we do this inside your office?" Valerie said, noting the department secretary and another student employee nearby within easy listening range.

"Works for me. This way."

A few minutes later, Finley looked up from the photograph Valerie had handed him, a grim expression on his face. "Poor girl. And, yes, I do know who she is." He looked at Luca. "I'm going to have to say her name. Is that okay with you?" he added, obviously familiar with Navajo fears concerning the recently deceased.

Luca nodded.

"This is—was—Lea Begay, a young Navajo woman who was enrolled in my survey course, Anthropology 101. With a lecture hall full of students I ordinarily wouldn't know her name, but she and I had a private conference a few weeks ago."

"And she wasn't happy with the outcome of your meeting," Valerie concluded, recalling the written comment Lea had made.

"How'd you know?" Finley asked, then, not waiting for an answer, continued. "She was having trouble with a class and wanted to drop out before her current grade could go into her records. She was afraid of losing her scholarship. As head of the department, I promised to bring up the matter with her professor."

As he spoke those last words, he didn't look at either of them, and that made Valerie suspect she wasn't getting the complete story. Glancing over at Luca, she saw he hadn't bought into it either.

"How far was she willing to push to get what she wanted?" Luca asked. "And did she end up making any enemies who were in a position to retaliate?"

"You mean like me? I barely knew the girl, and I never spent time with her except in class—and that one meeting. All I can tell you is that she didn't drop out of *my* lecture. It was Dr. Becenti's class that she was concerned about. Her friends or family might know more about that."

As if sensing something still left unsaid, Luca continued to press. "This Dr. Becenti... Is he around?"

"He's got class coming up at the top of the hour," Finley said, checking the schedule.

"What can you tell us about him?" Valerie asked.

"He's got a reputation for being a tough instructor. A lot of people, not just students, have had problems with him before."

"Like you?" Luca asked.

"Yeah, like me. But I'm just one of many." Finley took a deep breath then let it out again. "To give you an idea, last summer he went to the Rez to conduct research for a paper about some obscure tribal sect that traced its roots back to the Civil War. Although he's part Navajo, and that should have cut him some slack, he managed to get everyone ticked off at him." He shook his head then shrugged. "I don't know what it was, but *no one,* from tribal historians on down, would even meet with him. The lack of trust he generated cost him a substantial grant."

Several minutes later Valerie and Luca returned to the car. "We didn't get the whole story on Lea...the victim," she said, quickly correcting herself. "Did you see how he deflected and talked about Becenti instead?" Valerie asked as she climbed behind the wheel. "According to the person I spoke to when I first called, Finley had nothing on his schedule when we were chasing the suspect around the apartment buildings."

"We should check out Dr. Finley's background and see if he has alibis that'll account for his time during either of the murders. He's obviously familiar with Navajo customs, and he knew one of a hundred and fifty students by name. He also arrived here after a hot, sweaty bike ride—and maybe a run across a roof or two earlier in the day. It could all be coincidence, but it merits a closer look."

"Those apartments near where we found the body are only a few miles east of the campus. He would have had plenty of time to ditch the sweatshirt and binoculars," Valerie said, backing out of the parking space. "Finley appears fit, is younger than I expected and the victim was a pretty young woman. I'm going to have a deputy dig deep into the good doctor's background—and have officers speak to everyone in the victim's classes."

"What about this Professor Becenti? He's in a position to know something about the victim—and Dr. Finley," Luca suggested. "Should we go back and track him down?"

"He's supposed to be teaching a class right now. Let's catch up to him later," Valerie said.

"Okay. In the meantime, how about showing me the other crime scene?"

"Good idea. The first murder took place out in the county near an irrigation ditch."

"So either our killer likes changes of scenery or he's been targeting specific victims and the murders aren't random," Luca said.

"We'll be looking for commonalities between vic one and two, but for now all I know for sure is that they both looked alike—same general description—hair color, height and weight and so on."

Valerie took the freeway. "You okay if I make a stop to change? I got something sticky on my blouse when I slid down the pipe chasing the hooded perp."

"Sure."

Within minutes they arrived at her apartment.

She lived beside a small city park less than a mile west from I-25. Six units stood side by side, all part of a reconverted pueblo-style mansion in an old section of the city. The parking area that surrounded it was nearly empty at the moment.

"Most my neighbors work and are almost never home. Then again, neither am I," she added with a shrug.

As they entered through the front door, boxes of all sizes and shapes greeted them. One coffee cup with the three little pigs emblazoned on it had been left on top of a large box next to an easy chair. A television stood about four feet in front of it against the wall.

"Just moved in?" he asked.

"Sorta—two months ago. Like I said, I'm never home." She crossed the small living room and headed to the bedroom. "I'll be back in a second."

Valerie stepped into the bedroom and closed the door behind her. There were more clothes on the floor than in the closet or drawers—meaning laundry day was long overdue. She hadn't had a chance to do more than rinse out a few things in the bathroom sink for the past two weeks. Grabbing one of the few remaining clean shirts from the closet, she hurried back out to meet Luca and found him at the kitchen sink, his hand cupped beneath the faucet.

"Need something?" she asked.

He sipped the water in his hand. "I just wanted a drink," he said, then dried his hand on a paper towel. "I couldn't find any glasses."

"I haven't unpacked them. I use the Dixie cups," she said, handing him a three-inch cup. "They were on sale," she added with a sheepish smile. "See, the thing is I generally don't have visitors. When I come home it's just to sleep."

Valerie knew she was talking too much. She often did that around people she didn't know well. With so little idle time in her life, her socializing skills stunk. Yet, all things considered, there was no place she'd rather be than hip deep in a case. That was where she excelled.

As Luca entered the cluttered living room, he stopped by the sideboard and reached behind it. A small, broken picture frame was lodged between that piece of furniture and the wall. "Remnants of an old boyfriend?" he asked, fishing it out.

She looked at him in surprise, and laughed, seeing what he was holding. "No boyfriends—old or new. That was undoubtedly left by the previous tenant." As a kid living with a single mom she'd learned one thing—happily-ever-afters didn't exist. Everything came with an expiration date—relationships, jobs and even people.

By the time they walked out of her apartment, the sun was low in the sky and sinking fast. "I can take you to the crime scene, but it'll be dark soon. I doubt we'll be able to see much."

"What was the victim's time of death?" he asked.

"Around nine at night, according to the M.E."

"This time of year that means it took place just after it got dark. The murder was premeditated, so he probably arrived earlier and waited for her to pass by. I'd like to go over there now and see the place as he did, at around the time the crime went down."

"This guy felt safe enough at both places to stick around and set the stage, too. That means he must have spent some serious time selecting each site."

"My guess is that long before the crimes went down, he checked out traffic patterns, people who live in the area and maybe even introduced himself to some of them as, say, a prospective home buyer, so they wouldn't get suspicious seeing him around."

"Sometimes serial killers will pose as utility workers, too, so keep that in mind as we poke around the area," she said. "We'll check out the first site then, afterward, we'll get you settled in somewhere."

"Can you recommend a motel close to your place? It'll make things easier since we'll be riding together."

"The apartment next door to mine is empty for now since my landlord plans to have the place completely repainted. It's convenient, but the walls are paper-thin," she said, then with a quick grin added, "If you snore, the deal's off."

"Take the risk and find out for yourself."

His low, husky voice teased her, and a shiver touched the base of her spine. The problem with Luca was that mystery clung to him like a second skin, and her imagination, always up to a challenge, was filling in the gaps in all sorts of interesting ways.

She switched off the ignition. "I'll tell you what. Get your bag from the back. We can get the key from the landlord. We'll leave your stuff here, then be on our way."

A short time later she unlocked the apartment door adjacent to hers and showed him in. With no boxes lying about it looked roomier than hers, though they were exactly the same size.

"A word of warning—hot water's in demand each morning," she said, almost as an afterthought. "In other words, move fast or you're liable to run out in the middle of a shower."

He quickly placed his duffel bag on the couch then met her by the door. "Okay, let's get going."

She blinked. She'd fully expected a crack about conserving water. Most of the men she knew would have considered it a matter of macho honor.

No matter how she looked at it, Luca wasn't like anyone she'd ever known. He was quiet control and vibrant sexiness all rolled into one exciting package.

Valerie locked the door and gave the key to Luca. As she turned around, their eyes suddenly met. The intensity mirrored in his gaze spoke to her without the need for words, awakening something nameless deep inside her.

Valerie tore her gaze from his quickly and headed to the car without looking back. The man was Big Trouble. No doubt about it.

Chapter Five

"What's it like, your home that is?" she asked as they got underway.

"It's west of Shiprock in the foothills below the mountains, among the piñons and junipers. Very quiet—no traffic sounds—just the crickets at night and an occasional howl from a coyote. Once in a while a jet passes by, very high, but my closest neighbor is about ten miles away."

"All that quiet's got to be nerve-racking. How can you stand it?"

He laughed. "It seems to me that cars racing by, honking horns and the wail of emergency vehicles would be far worse. And there's railroad tracks just a few miles to the west. How do you ever get any sleep?" he countered.

"I guess it all comes down to what you're used to," she said after a beat.

As she thought about the place he'd described, she suppressed a shudder. Just her and her thoughts? No, thanks. She'd had enough days like that as a kid. Every time they'd moved to a new town she'd spent hours alone, wondering if she should even bother making new friends. Her mom and she had never stayed anyplace for long. Back then the silence of her room had been her only constant companion.

Thinking back, something she generally avoided doing, made Valerie realize how far she'd come. These days, police

The earth beneath their feet was hard packed where the service vehicles had formed tracks and sandy elsewhere except on the ditch banks themselves. Valerie studied the area as they drew near. She'd expected a slew of footprints from curious onlookers. Yet it was clear that ditch-bank joggers had veered to either side of the smoothed over area, now covered with a few inches of relocated sand. Nothing else marked the site, not even a rustic wooden cross. Those were typically left behind in New Mexico whenever a death had occurred, especially on long rural highways.

"A Navajo family lives close by," he said.

She blinked. "That's entirely possible. As I said, this is a mixed neighborhood." Valerie looked down at the footprints, trying to guess how he'd been able to tell.

"They live over there," he said, pointing with his lips. "The closest house to the ditch."

"How do you know? Moccasin prints?"

"Like in a John Wayne western?" he asked, laughing. "Naw, it's the home cooking. Don't you smell the fry bread and mutton stew?"

She sniffed the air and got nothing except the vague scent of what might have been *sopaipillas*. Or maybe that was just wishful thinking since she'd skipped lunch and had a craving for a big combo plate from Maria's.

"We should approach from the front of the house," she said. "They're probably a little jumpy around here, and people in the county often have a gun in the closet."

"Here's the way," he said, pointing out the best route, which was still visible though the sun had finally set.

Valerie followed as he led the way down the ditch bank along an obviously well-traveled foot trail. The man had incredible senses.

As they reached the end of a dirt road that led away from the river, she made a call to the station and soon had the information she wanted. "None of the locals our deputies interviewed stated they were Navajo."

"I'm not surprised that local Navajo families made themselves scarce. Like me, most dislike speaking of the dead."

They walked a half block to reach the house backed up to the ditch bank and read the address on the mailbox. Valerie called it in and after getting the information she needed, closed up the phone. "Rita and John Tsosie are the listed occupants, but no one was home when our deputies checked. Officers have come by twice since then but no luck so far."

He nodded, then stopped at the end of the sidewalk that led to their front porch. Valerie brushed past him. "I saw movement. Somebody's definitely inside," she said.

Before he could stop her, she knocked on the door, identifying herself loudly.

Hearing the slamming of a door by the side of the house, Valerie ran over to a sedan parked beneath a carport. A Navajo man and woman were getting into the vehicle.

"Sheriff's Department. Stop right there," she ordered. "Out of the car, please, sir, ma'am."

The couple froze and stared at her.

"I'm Detective Valerie Jonas with the Bernalillo County Sheriff's Department. I need to ask you a few questions," she said, hearing Luca coming up.

The man and woman stared blankly at her.

"We need your help to catch a killer. A young woman was murdered on the ditch bank not far from your house and—" She saw pure horror flash in their eyes, and both stepped away from her, moving down the driveway. Sure they were going to bolt, Valerie added, "Just stay put. Nobody thinks you had anything to do with this, but we need your help. Navajo witchcraft was involved—"

The woman gave a startled cry and the man, taking her hand, edged even farther away from Valerie.

"Please just go away, Officer. We don't know anything," he said. "We can't help you."

"Yáat'ééh," Luca greeted. "I apologize. We should have

waited to be invited to approach, though things are different here away from the *Dinétah.*

"I'm Detective Luca Nakai of the Navajo Tribal Police," he said, using the name only because it was a necessity. "My clan is *Dibé łizhiní.* I was born for *k'aahanáanii.*"

"I'm from the Black Sheep People, also." John Tsosie glanced down at Luca's special medicine pouch. "I know your father, the *hataalii.* Is he the reason you were chosen to come help the police here?"

He nodded. "The one who's been causing so much trouble needs to be caught soon, Uncle," Luca said.

Valerie immediately smiled. "You should have told me he's your uncle."

Luca shook his head. "We're not related. It's a term we use to show respect," he answered.

Valerie clamped her mouth shut. It was hard for her to take a backseat in an investigation but, here, her way had gotten them nowhere. Forcing herself to remain silent—which was as difficult for her as giving up chocolate—she watched Luca and listened closely.

"Did you see anything unusual the night of the killing?" Luca asked Rita.

"I heard something outside while I was cleaning up in the kitchen. It was the evil one at work," the woman said in a hushed whisper. "We have protection," she said, pointing to her *jish,* "but we'll still be leaving soon to have an Enemy Way."

"So you saw the guilty one?" Luca pressed.

Mrs. Tsosie hesitated. "He was only an outline in the moonlight, but I saw enough to know what he was."

She'd said *what* not *who,* Valerie noted. When Rita lapsed into another long silence, Valerie could barely stand it. She was about to press her for an answer when Luca, noting it, shook his head. She bit her tongue and did her best.

An eternity later Mrs. Tsosie continued, her voice the merest of whispers. "He had a coyote animal skin over his head and back."

"Did you see his face at all?" Valerie asked immediately.

She shook her head. "It was dark, and his face was covered in shadows," Rita said softly.

"But you're sure he was using the skin of a coyote…not, say, a wolf or a big dog?" Luca asked softly.

"Yes, I'm sure. I've seen plenty of coyotes before. Right after that I closed all the windows and drew the curtains. My husband sat by the door with his rifle for about an hour, maybe longer. Afterward, we left to spend a few days at a relative's house over in *To'hajiilee*."

The small Navajo community in the county was west of Albuquerque. As Valerie considered what the woman had told them, she found herself growing more skeptical by the second. To her, it sounded more as if the woman were describing the stuff of her nightmares as opposed to anything real.

Luca looked from Rita to John. "I could do a *hozonji,* a song of blessing, for you," he said. "It'll bring peace to you and your home."

"Nephew, we would welcome that," John said.

Valerie looked at Luca, wondering what he had in mind. Then Luca's voice rose in a song that seemed to pulsate with its own power. It held the magic of antiquity and the soothing strength of a culture that had persevered against all odds.

Valerie could hear her heart drumming inside her chest as Luca finished the blessing. His song had wrapped itself around her and filled her with emotions she didn't dare define.

"Thank you, Nephew," John Tsosie said, his tone now more relaxed.

The Tsosies walked toward their home, then Rita stopped and focused on Valerie. "The one you're after is very dangerous," she said. "He can harm with nothing more than a touch. You don't believe in our ways but this evil is real."

"We won't give up until he's in custody, ma'am," Valerie assured, deliberately avoiding anyone's name.

"There are many ways of causing death," John Tsosie added, glancing around warily in the gathering gloom. "Listen to the *hataalii's* son," he added, indicating Luca. "He'll help you stay alive."

"I'm not going into this unprepared," she said with an encouraging smile, patting her holster. "A coyote skin isn't bulletproof."

She'd meant it to reassure them, but the couple shook their heads almost in unison then walked to the side door and stepped inside their house.

Valerie started to follow them inside, but Luca stopped her. "You're not welcome. You've been near a dead body without the proper wards."

"Then ask them to come back out. We're not finished."

"Yes, we are, at least for now. They've told you all they know."

"How can you be sure?"

"The man and I come from the same clan. He has no need to lie to me or hold back. We're connected through blood. Do you understand?"

Valerie didn't answer, having been lied to by relatives a lot closer than that.

As they walked back down the street, she thought about what had just happened. Even the timbre of Luca's voice seemed to hold an inexplicable power. Everything about him whispered to her to stop trying to explain the unexplainable and learn to accept mysteries that defied logic by their very existence.

Chapter Six

As they climbed into the police unit, Luca caught a whiff of the lavender scent she wore. The soft fragrance was in sharp contrast with the toughness she tried to project. Valerie was a maze of inconsistencies strung together and, like a squash blossom necklace, all the different facets combined into one beautiful whole.

He'd been attracted to many women during the course of his life, but what drew him to Valerie was too powerful to dismiss easily. He hadn't felt anything like this since…his beautiful Merilyn.

She'd meant everything to him and he'd intended on making her his wife. Then a senseless accident had suddenly taken her from him. Grief had held him in a stranglehold and he'd raged against fate for eighteen months. Then, slowly, he'd worked himself out of that valley of pain.

He'd been told that a heart scarred by a devastating loss is never the same, and for him, that was the case. That dark period had taught him lessons he'd never forget.

The Navajo Way held that everything had two sides. Now that he'd seen the dark side of love, he'd never walk down that path again. And certainly not with Valerie Jonas. She was all wrong for him. If he'd been searching for a mate—which he wasn't— he would have looked for a homebody, a soft, gentle spirit who would act as a counter to his warrior nature and balance him.

Yet despite logic, something about Valerie tugged at him, compelling him to look beyond her fiery toughness and see the woman she kept hidden from the world. But to do that would require more than just a tumble in bed, and therein lay the problem.

"When you mentioned clans back there, you said you were 'born' for one of them. What's that mean?" she asked, interrupting his thoughts as she drove back into the city.

"My clan is the same as my mother's. The clan I was 'born for,' the Living Arrow People, signifies my father's clan."

She said nothing for a few minutes, then added, "As partners we should get to know each other better, but everything about you is so different I don't even know where to start."

"Come inside the apartment with me," he said, throwing caution to the wind as something dark stirred inside him. "We'll learn until dawn." Seeing her shiver in response to his words, his body tightened.

"No," she managed in a strangled voice. Then, taking an unsteady breath, she added, "We both like playing with fire. It's part of our natures. But in this case, we could end up getting fried. Come over and get some clean sheets for your bed. Then we'll meet again early tomorrow morning."

Moments later she handed him a set of sheets and some towels. "Get some sleep, we'll need to leave here no later than eight. Shall I wake you up at seven?"

"Not necessary. I'll be up at dawn."

"Does your watch have an alarm?"

"No, I've got an internal clock that never fails me. I always wake up at dawn."

"Oookay, country boy," Valerie said with a smile. "I'll see you tomorrow." With a quick wave, she closed the door.

Taking a deep breath, he carried the things she'd given him into his apartment. The bare mattress in the bedroom looked singularly uninviting, but even after he made the bed he felt no compulsion to call it a night. Without Valerie, crawling between those sheets seemed pointless. He was too wound up to get any sleep. Maybe a shower would help him relax.

Luca stripped off his shirt and started to undo his jeans when he heard a noise somewhere behind him. He froze, recognizing the dry rattling sound. Turning only his head, and that very slowly, he spotted the small western diamondback snake. Uncoiling its black-and-white striped tail, the reptile slithered slowly across the hardwood floor, heading toward the darkness beneath the couch.

Luca took a steadying breath. He'd capture the snake, then take it someplace where it could be safely released. There was no need to kill it—providing he acted quickly.

The towels Valerie had given him were still within reach. In one fluid motion, he grabbed one from the stack and unfurled it as he tossed it over the rattler.

Luca stepped closer, carefully watching the movement beneath the towel. When the snake poked its head out from under the cloth, tongue flicking the air, Luca grabbed the diamondback just behind its head. It hissed and squirmed, attempting to coil, but it couldn't strike him now.

Keeping the snake at arm's length so it couldn't wrap around his wrist, Luca eyed the bronze-colored metal trash can in the corner. He could drop it in there, but he'd need to find something to work as a lid and the towel wouldn't do.

He glanced around the apartment, but found nothing that would serve to keep the snake securely inside, like a big plate. And that was only part of his problem. No matter what he ended up using, one thing was clear. He'd need an extra pair of hands—something to keep the lid in place while he pulled his hand back.

Keeping a firm but not harmful hold on the rattler, he knocked on the left wall of the apartment. Valerie was bound to hear him.

"I need your help," he said, pressing his head against the wall, remembering that she'd said they were paper-thin.

A moment later he heard a knock at his door. "You okay?"

"No. Yes. I'm opening the door, but stay cool."

Keeping the snake well away from his body, and wiggling it slightly to keep it from coiling upward toward his forearm, he unlocked the door then stepped back.

Valerie rushed in, gun in hand. The first thing she saw was Luca, shirtless. He was magnificent. His jeans were undone, too, and it was obvious he chose to forgo underwear.

Her breath lodged at the back of her throat and she lowered her gun. The bronzed muscles that rippled down his chest practically begged for a woman's touch. For a heart-stopping moment she wondered what it would be like to taste him, to run her tongue down the length of him.

Out of the corner of her eye, she grew aware that he appeared to be shaking a beaded rope.... Then, suddenly the rope moved on its own.

Valerie yelped and jumped back. "That's a *snake!*"

She *hated* snakes. Reptiles of any kind had always terrified her.

"Shall I shoot it?" she managed in a raspy voice, her throat completely dry.

"No. Snakes have their place. If I'd have wanted it dead, I wouldn't have called you over," he said calmly.

"Right. I'll call animal control," she said, looking around his room for the cell phone.

"Not necessary."

"So what would you like to do next?" she asked slowly.

Luca gestured to the trash can behind him. "Get that, then find something that'll fit securely over the top."

Valerie opened the drawer of the end table next to the sofa and pulled out the phone book. Hers had been kept in the same place. She then brought the trash can over and set it down on the floor beside him. With the phone book still in her hand, she watched him—and the snake—carefully. "You're going to drop the snake in the trash can, right? But what if it strikes you or me in the process?"

"It won't," he said firmly.

Ten seconds later, the snake was inside the can, blocked from escaping by the Albuquerque metropolitan phone directory, three inches thick. Luca had his hand on the top, keeping the snake from pushing the heavy volume away.

"I'm going to need you to hold the phone book in place for a moment," he said.

As he drew his hand back, she placed hers on the top, holding the directory secure.

Luca immediately reached for his shirt, slipped it on then fastened his jeans and belt.

"Now what?" she asked, keeping her hand firmly in place. "Are you planning to adopt this thing?"

"I'll keep the snake inside while you drive," he said, putting his socks and boots back on. "We'll set it free in the foothills, away from housing and people."

"We'll have to drive farther than just the foothills for that."

"Then we'd better get started."

They were in the unmarked sedan five minutes later. He was aware of the soft, clean scent of soap on her skin. She'd taken a shower before coming over. He wished he could have joined her….

That look on her face when she'd seen him shirtless and the way her hungry gaze had drifted down him had sparked a fire in his blood. Any man worth his salt knew when a woman wanted him. Though he tried to fight it, his body tensed and his mood darkened.

"Rattlesnakes in the city…it's not that common," she said slowly. "I've never seen one except in the *bosque* alongside the river."

"But it's not out of the realm of possibility, right?"

"No, but the odds are really against it. I'm thinking someone left you a present." She paused. "Which means we were followed when we left the crime scene—or maybe after our meeting with Finley."

"And that means we have an even bigger problem now," he said, finishing her thought. "We'll have to relocate."

"I've already got a place in mind but I'll have to check with the department."

As she called in and made a report, Luca thought about their situation. This wasn't his turf. The city…so many cars… Had he missed a tail? It didn't seem likely, but the facts supported a different conclusion. This woman was a constant distraction at a time when he could least afford to lose focus.

She glanced over, her eyes dipping downward. "That snake…. We're safe, right? No way it could jump out?"

"Everything will stay in place until we're ready," he answered, his voice very controlled and quiet.

For a moment, uncertain if he'd woven more than one meaning into his words, she said nothing and tried to ignore the way he could make her skin prickle with just one of his looks. Minutes stretched out.

"How come you're so intent on saving that snake?" she asked at last. "Rattlesnakes are nasty things. I had a partner who got bit when we were investigating a homicide up on La Luz Trail. It's not just the fangs or the poison that gets you. Tissue dies and then infections begin," she said, struggling to focus on something else besides Luca.

"The *Diné* believe that snakes represent the Lightning People and are related to Thunder. Killing one could drive away the rains, and then all life would go hungry."

"A snake's bite is nothing to shrug off either," she muttered, hearing it slithering around inside the trash can.

"Our stories tell us that First Man, First Woman and Coyote brought witchcraft with them when they came out from the underworld." His strong voice held a mesmeric quality that completely captivated her. "When First Woman began to hand out the power, snake had no pockets, so the only place he could store it was in his mouth. That's why the bite can kill."

"Snakes…and witchcraft…"

"It's very possible the evil we're after brought the snake over as a warning," he finished.

She nodded silently. Her ingrained caution popped suddenly into place as she felt the pull between them. The attraction was getting too strong too quickly. Luca and she belonged to different worlds, and nothing would ever change that. Wishing for the impossible had been her mother's mistake. She wouldn't repeat what could only lead to tears.

Valerie focused on the road beyond the headlights as they turned off the interstate. The two-lane road leading south would take them into the foothills of the Manzano Mountains.

Ten minutes later, after passing the ranger station, she pulled off the road and parked. The forest came right up to the highway and no buildings or lights were within sight.

"How about here?" she asked.

"It'll do. I'll take the snake about fifty yards into the forest, then release it by some boulders."

She came around to open the door and he climbed out, still holding the snake in the makeshift container.

"Wait here," he said, then walked slowly into the trees, picking his way carefully in the moonlight.

He came back several minutes later, carrying the trash can with the phone book inside. "It's finished," he said, placing the objects on the backseat then climbing into the car.

"Not quite. That link between witchcraft and the snake cinched it for me. We're relocating to a safe house. I've already cleared things with the department."

They stopped at their apartments long enough to get their things, and then, after searching the car for tracking devices and finding none, they set out.

"This safe house we're going to is only a few blocks from the station." She glanced in the rearview mirror, checking for a tail. "He won't find us again—that's, of course, assuming that he actually did put the snake in the apartment and it didn't just crawl in there on its own. It's possible, since it was a young one, that some crazy person decided to keep it as a pet and it escaped."

Luca nodded, but said nothing. One thing was clear to him. He'd never lower his guard again, even for an instant.

An hour later, after driving around the city until both felt completely sure they hadn't been followed, Valerie pulled into the well-lit parking lot of a former high school. The historic brick building had been extensively remodeled and converted into spacious upscale, loft-style apartments.

"We'll be on the third floor," she told him. "There are cameras in the parking lot and lobby, and someone from the department will monitor us whenever we're here."

He glanced around. What she considered safe showcased the differences between them. To her, safety was found five minutes from city hall, amid the traffic and under streetlights. He would have preferred his own *Dinétah* where they could have stayed out in the open, atop a rock-strewn mesa. It would have been impossible for anyone to approach them there without announcing their presence.

"You don't like it here, I can tell. But why not?" she asked. "It's practically impregnable. And we're close to the department. Backup can be here in two minutes or less."

He nodded slowly. That was an undeniable advantage. On the Rez, backup was sometimes hours away and officers usually worked alone. "No matter how impregnable it appears to be, I'd still like to put up some wards."

"Sure. Do whatever makes you comfortable. But keep in mind that it's already two in the morning and we'll have to get an early start tomorrow," she said, stifling a yawn.

Valerie led the way to the entrance, and after showing her badge to the man behind the glass door in the lobby they were allowed inside.

As they walked across the gleaming hardwood floor, Luca studied the security measures in place. Cameras covered every angle in the lobby. A second security guard, in a locked room, looked up from the monitors behind the reinforced glass window and nodded as they walked by.

As far as safety, it had been a good choice. Yet the threat

facing them was rooted in the old ways, deadly and able to employ strategies and powers that transcended the gun and the locked door. Although Valerie had the heart of a warrior this wasn't her kind of fight—it was his.

Chapter Seven

Luca was up before dawn. Moving silently, he checked all the wards he'd placed around the apartment the night before. Though burglar alarms protected each window, he'd added prayersticks, War plants and special powders at all points of entry. He'd also reinforced the front door with Talking Rock Medicine. No skinwalker would be able to successfully challenge those wards—and two armed officers.

When the sun started to peer over the Sandia Mountains, Luca went out into the tiny balcony that faced the courtyard. While much of the city still slept, he offered pollen to the Dawn, invoking Sun's protection. As the pollen grains caught in the gentle breeze, he felt, rather than saw, Valerie behind him. Turning, he wished her good morning.

She held out a cup of coffee. "I made it strong. I figure we both needed a big kick this morning."

"Thanks."

"There's something I'd like you to see. I've got it up on my laptop right now. The morning paper ran a story about the crimes—and you. It doesn't identify you by name, but it indicates that your father is the revered *hataalii* who blessed the new Tribal Council chambers a month ago. The reporter also mentions that the department called you in to consult because of the Navajo ritualistic components found at both crime scenes."

She led the way to the marble desk against the south wall

and pointed to her laptop computer. "That's the electronic version of the story."

Luca read it, then sat back. Though there was only a vague reference to it, the reporter had also picked up on the circle of flames symbol and its significance to the Brotherhood. No details had been given, but the fact that the reporter had known about the Brotherhood at all bothered him. "Has anyone spoken to this reporter to see how he or she is getting these facts?"

"We had an officer visit the newspaper, but freedom of the press and all that makes it tricky. The paper hasn't given the reporter a byline, so we can't narrow down his identity just yet. The editor in chief claims that the reporter put things together with the help of sources, but the paper's steadfastly refusing to reveal those to us."

"Maybe someone in the anthropology department at the university provided help," Luca suggested, scanning the article again. "Doctor Finley perhaps, or Becenti."

"It's possible," she said with a nod.

He leaned back and stared off across the room, lost in thought. "I need to make a call," he said at last, placing his empty coffee cup down.

"Why don't you use the cell phone I gave you?"

"Great, thanks." He stepped out of the combination kitchen/living room and went into the bedroom he'd occupied the night before. Closing the door to give himself additional privacy, he called *Diné Nééz,* his contact in the Brotherhood, and updated him. The Albuquerque paper was distributed across the state and the article had already been noticed back on the Rez.

"The connection to us is disturbing, Cougar. Dismiss it in the eyes of others, at least as much as possible," *Diné Nééz* said, then paused for several moments. "From everything you've told me, these crimes fit the work of an evil one, but your tone of voice tells me you're not convinced."

"The crimes seem out of place here, so far from tribal

land, and the first victim wasn't Navajo. Instinct tells me there's more to what's happening than meets the eye, but I don't have any clear answers yet."

"We won't be far if you need us. There are Brotherhood warriors in the city who can help you at a moment's notice."

"There's one more thing I need for my partner," Luca said, then explained. Once the request was made, Luca hung up. The figure in the hooded sweatshirt… They'd initially thought of him as someone implicated in the crime, but they might have been dealing with an undercover reporter working a story—someone out to protect his identity.

Hearing a knock, he turned his head as Valerie stepped into the room.

"Time to go."

"I've been thinking of the man in the hooded sweatshirt."

"Me, too," Valerie said. "He may have been the reporter trying to get more details for the morning edition."

"If that's who he is, he'll find us again," Luca said.

"Did you notice that part about the killings being a direct challenge to a special faction on the reservation? The Brotherhood of Warriors, the reporter called it."

He nodded. "From what I've heard, that group came into being during the time of Kit Carson, then faded away— the stuff of legends, you know? What concerns me more is the mention of the buckskin strips found at the site. He would have had to come *very* close to the body to identify those. That reporter may have been at the crime scene before we were."

"All the footprints on the inside of the yard have been accounted for, but there were a bunch in the alley. Several people had a look from over the wall before the scene was cordoned off," Valerie said. "Since some reporters have police scanners, it's not impossible he got there before APD. Let me call in and have the crime scene photos taken of the crowd sent to my computer. We may get something that way—if he hung around."

A few minutes later, Luca once again sat with her at the computer, studying photos of the crowd. "I don't see anyone with a hooded sweatshirt," he said at last. "Or carrying a jacket or sweatshirt either."

"Neither do I," she admitted. "A few of the students have book bags that could hold one, but I don't see anyone who's the size and shape of the hooded guy we're looking for."

"Can you pull up close-up photos of the two victims so they're side by side? I'd like to compare them."

She pressed a few keystrokes, then slid the computer over in front of him. "There they are—one and two."

He leaned forward as he clicked the mouse and zoomed in. "One of the trademarks of a skinwalker is that he acts counter to the ways we're taught to honor. The slash marks on both victims indicate that they had their throats cut from east to west. That's the exact opposite of the method we use for butchering sheep. All good gifts come from the east, so we make the cut from west to east. Also, instead of catching the blood like we do with our animals, so nothing's wasted, he allowed it to spill freely and contaminate the earth."

"Contaminate how?" she asked.

"The *Diné* are one with the earth. But by spilling his victim's blood this way, the evil one poisons the soil with anger and fear. Food that springs from tainted earth poisons our minds, and allows cycles of hatred to be repeated."

"And repeated they will be. This type of killer won't stop until he's behind bars."

"Mr. Hooded Shirt is connected to our investigation," Luca said, his hand resting on his medicine bundle. "Reporter or killer—we need to find out which."

"And we will." She turned off her laptop and stood. "Right now you and I are going back to the scene of the second murder to canvass the area. It's Saturday, so we may catch people who weren't around to be interviewed before. With luck, one of them will give us a lead."

THEY ARRIVED on-site less than twenty minutes later and parked in the small lot of a strip mall one block off Central. "I say we walk around first and get a feel for the neighborhood. Hooded Shirt might even live around here," Valerie said.

"While we walk, we can listen, too," he said, gesturing Navajo-style toward a group of perhaps ten teenage boys across the street. They were in the alley behind a small Mexican restaurant, gathered around a white sedan that had been modified as a lowrider. One of the teens was talking to another young man in a white shirt standing on the restaurant's small loading dock.

"Heads up, partner. Those kids belong to one of the most violent gangs in the area, the Skulls," she said, meeting the gaze of a young member who'd noticed Valerie and Luca crossing the street. "We'll need to cover each other's backs here. These punks like to mix it up with cops."

Just then the boy in the white shirt jumped down into the crowd. All of the others rushed forward, punching and kicking him as he fell to the ground.

"Looks like a ranking. Let's go," she said.

Making sure her badge was in plain sight, she reached the closest boy and swung him out of the way. "Everyone, back off!" she ordered.

"This is private," another boy shouted, grabbing her arm. "We don't need no cops."

"Get your hand off me before I break it," she snapped.

She then reached for another kid, one she recognized. Chico Ramirez ran the Skulls. Chico whirled around, brushing away her hand and brandishing a knife with a four-inch blade. "Come on, witch. Take it away, I dare you."

Luca, who'd arrived unnoticed, grabbed the boy's knife hand then pressed down with his thumb. The knife dropped out of Chico's hand and hit the ground with a clunk.

"We use kitchen knives like those for slicing peaches," Luca said, his tone icy cold. "If you want to carry a fighting knife, you need something with a little more reach." He bent down, then pulled out a seven-inch commando knife from a sheath inside his boot. The double-edged blade looked razor sharp. "Wanna know what I had to do to earn those notches?"

Silence followed as the boys stared at the sawtooth grooves near the upper edge of the blade, right below the hasp.

"My warrior ancestors did some crazy things to earn the notches on their flint blades. These days our daggers are tempered steel, so the work's easier now. Progress, huh?" he added with a sadistic grin.

The boys stepped away and looked over at Chico.

"We're done here," Ramirez said, kicking his dropped knife toward one of the other boys, who stooped and picked it up.

In a flurry of movement the boys scattered, running in several directions. As they did, the injured teen on the ground slowly got to his knees and wiped the blood off his cheek with his sleeve.

"Don't move," Valerie ordered, crouching next to the injured boy and noting the swelling just below his left eye. "I'll call the paramedics."

"No. It'll make things worse." With effort he stood. Waving away her offer of a helping hand, he leaned against the side rail of the loading dock, catching his breath.

"What's your name?" Valerie asked.

"Joe Chavez," he managed, his breathing raspy.

"What happened?" Valerie asked him.

"Getting ranked in means you've got to be tested and prove you've got what it takes."

"You should come up with a better future for yourself— one that'll keep you out of the morgue and/or jail." Seeing the way he was holding his side, she softened her tone and added, "You really should let me call the paramedics. Another kick and you'd have lost an eye. And your ribs might be broken."

"I can take it. The Skulls need me—someone who can slip in and out of places without being seen."

Valerie picked up on his tone of voice and decided to play a hunch. "Okay, just what did you see that's so important?"

He hesitated.

"Hey. You owe us one," Luca said, then added in a slow voice, "Gang members on the Rez honor things like that. It's the mark of a man."

Valerie glanced at Luca, biting back a reply. Good ol' boy ethics always made her gag. Yet as she looked back at the boy, she realized that Luca was getting through to him.

"If you want, we can take you into custody. That should impress your crew," Luca added.

"Yeah, okay," he said. "But how about just cuffing me for a while, then letting me go when we're done? I've got to get cleaned up and go to work. Deal?"

"You've got it, kid," Valerie said, bringing out her hand-cuffs. As she secured his hands behind his back, the boy groaned loudly.

"You okay?" Valerie asked him instantly.

"Yeah, just making it look good," he whispered as she turned him around. "You never know who's watching."

"Okay, Joe. We've played along. Now it's your turn," Valerie said.

"This is Skulls turf, and around here nobody does anything to disrespect that," he said in a voice that was barely above a whisper. "But one night about a week ago, I got off work late and saw this weird-looking man wandering around. He was carrying one of those folding shovels—the old G.I. kind like my granddad has. I decided to follow him and saw him go to the empty lot behind the apartment building. We all have stuff there, but this guy wasn't from our hood, and he sure wasn't acting right."

Valerie shook her head. "Slow down. You're losing me. What's the deal with the empty lot?"

"It started a few years ago when Mrs. Sanchez's Chihua-hua died. She loved that old dog and didn't want to just dump it in the trash, but she lived in the apartments up the street.

So she buried it in the empty lot behind there and put a cross on the grave. Then Allison Perea's cat got run over, and it went there, too. Pretty soon the whole place was like a pet cemetery. Even the Skulls have animals there. Chico's pit bull was buried there last month."

"So you told Chico what you'd seen—which was what?" Valerie pressed.

"Someone not from our hood digging up the old graves, then burying everything back again. Is that nuts or what? At first I thought he was robbing graves, but for what—dog collars?" He shrugged. "It made no sense, but the dude came back two nights in a row."

"So what was he taking—body parts?" Luca asked.

"Beats me. He'd uncover the skeletons, reach in then bury the whole thing again. After I told Chico about it, he had us staking out the cemetery. We caught him at it, but before we could grab the guy, he took off. I've never seen anyone run so fast in my life. Nobody even got close."

"Have you seen him since?" Valerie asked.

The boy shook his head.

"What was the guy wearing?" Luca asked him.

"A baggy sweatshirt and jeans."

"Did you ever see his face?" Valerie pressed.

Joe shook his head. "That was the weird part. The guy kept the hood on, even when he was digging. All I can tell you for sure is that he was bigger than me, maybe your size," he said, indicating Luca.

"Thanks," Valerie said, then brought out her business card.

"Drop it on the ground," he said, "in case somebody is still watching. And shove me around a little before you take off the cuffs, okay?"

"Glad to help, Joe. Just give me a call if you think of anything else," Valerie added, then shoved him back against the wall, spun him around roughly and removed the cuffs.

"Take off, punk!" she snapped loudly.

He mad dogged her a second, cringing from the bump

beside his eye, then opened the door to the restaurant and ducked inside.

As he disappeared from view, Luca turned around slowly.

Valerie tensed up immediately. "What's up?"

"We're being watched. Can't you feel it?"

Automatically, she reached down and unsnapped the holster strap that kept her gun in place. "By now everyone knows we're cops and we're here asking questions. It's not unusual for people in high-crime areas to start watching us. Neighbors call other neighbors, warning them."

"It's not just curiosity. It's something…more."

"Then let's walk a bit," she said, not liking the prospect of becoming a stationary target. "Maybe they'll show themselves."

In some inner-city neighborhoods, Valerie knew that people scattered or turned away when the police were about, many times simply in fear of looking like an informant and becoming a victim of retaliation. She peered into the shadows around the buildings and, taking a page from Luca's book, looked at the pigeons. Nothing.

Luca fell into step beside her and they went down the now-deserted sidewalk. Five minutes later they arrived at a small park beside a busy street. Ahead they saw a mounted police officer she recognized as Tim Murphy. Valerie walked over and smiled, petting the horse. "Hey, Murph. And how you doing, Dr. Pepper?" she asked the horse softly.

Murphy dismounted and joined them on foot. "More trouble?" he asked, keeping his voice low, watching the park and not the street beside him.

"Not so far," Valerie answered in an equally soft voice. "But what are you doing here? Don't you normally patrol that big park over by Veteran's Hospital?"

Hearing the sounds of unusually heavy traffic, she turned her head and looked up and down the street. "Something going on today?" she asked.

"Some Washington hotshots are giving some foreign guests a tour of the base and the labs, and they're going to be coming out the Truman gate. Their route will take them down this way. That's why Pepper and I are here—lending support to the motorcade by watching for troublemakers." He glanced around. "But nothing's scheduled to begin for another hour. I'm going to get myself a soft drink at Tamura's." He motioned toward a mom-and-pop grocery store just north of the park, which occupied less than a city block. "You want one?"

"No, thanks."

Officer Murphy led the horse over to the park sign, then tied the reins loosely to the metal post. He waved to Valerie, then jogged off toward the store.

Valerie turned to Luca, who was still gazing off into the distance, back in the direction they'd come. "You're starting to creep me out. What's bothering you? Are we being followed again?"

To the south, beside another small park adjacent to an elementary school, a man was coiling a length of chain that had just been used to tow a broken-down car. He dropped the chain into the bed of a pickup with a thunk, then walked over to the hood of the car where another man was working on the engine.

"Don't look now, but we're being watched from across the street," Luca said in a whisper. "I saw a flash—like maybe from binoculars—behind that purple plum tree next to the gas station."

Valerie turned slowly, looking up as a passenger jet from the airport to the south roared into the sky. Casually turning east, she spotted a shape beside the ornamental tree. In an instant the person turned away, put something into a large bag then strode away briskly in the opposite direction.

Assuming Luca would be right behind her, Valerie sprinted across the four-lane thoroughfare and raced down the residential street. She was running as fast as she could but had been unable to see anything except the back of the man trying to get away. At the moment, he was gaining ground on her and it looked like he might get away.

Hearing the sound of galloping hooves approaching from behind, she turned her head. "Catch him, Murph!" she called out.

Valerie suddenly realized the rider wasn't Murphy. It was Luca, and his eyes were locked on their fleeing suspect.

Chapter Eight

Valerie veered to the side, giving Luca and his mount plenty of room. The suspect heard the hoofbeats approaching, swerved back toward the street then cut back between parked cars onto a lawn.

Glancing back over his shoulder, the man missed seeing the sprinkler on the lawn. He tripped and fell facedown onto the wet grass, sliding for several feet.

Luca reined in Pepper, slowing to a trot and circling around the man on the grass, blocking his way. "Stay down," Luca ordered, "or get stomped. Your choice."

"No problem, man. I'm too tired to run anymore," the man groaned, rolling onto his back and extending his arms out away from his body.

Pepper, a seasoned officer, stopped and held his ground as Luca dismounted.

"Hold it right there, buddy," Valerie said, running up to cover Luca, her pistol pointed at the suspect. The man looked vaguely familiar to her but she couldn't place him.

"No need for the gun, I'm unarmed and I'm not going anywhere," the man said, still breathing hard. "Okay, maybe I shouldn't have run, but give me a break. I'm working on a story here."

He sat up, brushing wet leaves and blades of grass off his sports jacket. "You're the police, after a killer—I'm a reporter, after the story."

"Let's see your press credentials," Valerie snapped. "Slowly."

As the man reached into his jacket pocket, Valerie saw Luca watching the man's eyes, ready to step in. Her partner's gaze revealed absolutely nothing, and coupled with that unearthly stillness of his, Luca came across as a walking danger zone.

Valerie took the man's wallet and, brushing away some slender, wiry leaves, looked inside. "Stephen Browning. The name sounds familiar, but I don't see any press card or ID here," she said. "Nothing but a university ID and parking permit."

Valerie relaxed slightly, tossing the wallet over to Luca. *Now* she remembered where she'd seen him. He'd come into the anthropology office when they'd been there. As she put her gun away, Valerie also noted that he was taller than Hooded Shirt.

"The guy who came into the anthropology office while we were there. Steve, right?" Luca confirmed.

"I teach journalism at the college," he said. "My name's Stephen Browning. You recognize me from television now?"

She shook her head.

"Sure you do! I used to cover the news for Channel 13 until I was arrested inside the gate at the base. Some nonsense about needing a pass—I was a reporter, for Pete's sake. A C-130 had crashed on takeoff and rumor had it that it was carrying radioactive materials. Of course there was a big cover-up, and I got caught in the middle. In order to keep me from the real story, base security locked me up for twenty-four hours. They dropped the charges the next day, but by then the news was all over the local channels. And lucky me, I got fired for just trying to do my job."

Now she remembered. Officially, Browning had gotten caught trying to sneak onto the base. "If you're teaching journalism these days, what are you doing here?"

"Proving I've still got what it takes to break a big story," he answered instantly. "I follow my gut and do whatever it takes to get to the truth. That lead article in today's paper was mine. I didn't get the byline yet, but I'll earn that soon enough."

"Why did you run when we spotted you tailing us?" Luca

asked, holding on to the reins of the horse and stroking its neck gently.

"I was afraid I'd get arrested. I've been following you two for a while. But here's the deal. This story's mine, and I'm *not* backing off. Arrest me if you want. I've got a lawyer."

"How did you come up with all the details of the crime scene?" Valerie pressed. "You seem very knowledgeable— almost too much so," she added, an edge to her voice.

"I'm not the killer if that's what you're thinking, but I do have top-notch sources," he said, his voice flat.

"I wonder how your Navajo sources would feel if they knew you were hanging around the dead," Luca said, shutting Browning's wallet and handing it back to him.

"How do you know my sources are Navajo?" Browning asked, his eyes narrowed.

"I'm not wrong," Luca responded.

"Give me a reason not to throw you in jail for interfering with a criminal investigation," Valerie said. "We know you were at the second crime scene before we arrived." It had been a shot in the dark, but his reaction told her she'd scored a direct hit.

"Look, just so you know I'm on your side, I'm going to give you a freebie," he said, not admitting or denying the allegation. "Lea Begay's best friend is a woman by the name of Mae Nez. She lives up in Tijeras Canyon."

Luca nodded once, his face impassive, and didn't comment. Valerie followed his lead, waiting but not saying a word. Not speaking seemed to spur Browning into making conversation. Maybe it was because television reporters were often natural extroverts and valued speaking—and being the center of attention—over listening.

"Mae knew Lea really well. She's your best bet if you want to get to know more about the second victim." He looked at Valerie, then at Luca. "Don't say I never gave you anything."

"Okay, thanks for the tip," Valerie said, nodding once. "But here's a heads-up for you, Browning. If you're going to tail an officer, don't hide in the shadows. Stay out in the open, and never—ever—run from us."

"Okay, but just so we're clear, I'll be right behind you guys every step of the way on this, so get used to it. You can't arrest me for sharing the same space."

"True—to a point. But trespass onto a crime scene or tamper with evidence and you'll be looking at jail time," she warned.

"I hear you." His gaze fastened on Luca, who hadn't said a word. "Man, you need to work on your people skills."

When Luca continued to look at him, Browning backed up a step then hurried away in the direction of the park.

They headed back after that, Luca leading Dr. Pepper this time. Valerie glanced over at him. "Those long silences of yours are really effective in police work," Valerie said. "You'll have to teach me that technique. No—never mind. I don't think I could pull it off. It's just not my style."

His mouth twitched but he never cracked a smile as they walked down the residential street.

"What made you so sure Browning's sources are Navajo?" she asked.

"Remember when he took his wallet out and you brushed away those leaves?"

"Yeah, the guy slid halfway across the lawn. So what?"

"Those didn't just come from the grass. I recognized the plant. My guess is that they spilled out of a medicine bundle that a Navajo woman gave him. It's not a common plant to carry around and has special significance. That's what tipped me off."

She waited for him to continue, but as the seconds ticked by she just couldn't stand it anymore. "You give new meaning to the term silent type. Are you planning to tell me the rest before nightfall?" she prodded with a grin.

He chuckled softly. "Everybody expects instant answers, like a television game show. Faster isn't always smarter. In the city, there's way too much talking and not enough thinking."

She could have argued the point. Her biggest problem was

that every time she was alone with Luca, her thoughts became X-rated.

"The leaves were from the yucca plant, the state flower, by the way. Our creation stories say that the Holy Beings rubbed yucca over the hearts of Man and Woman and that's what caused them to fall in love."

"Handy little plant," she said with a playful smile.

A few seconds later Murphy came jogging up to meet them. He gave Luca a surprised look. "I've got to hand it to you. You sure have a way around horses. I'm surprised Pepper didn't buck you off. He has a tendency to do that to riders he doesn't know."

"I've never had problems with horses. We always seem to connect," he said, handing the officer the reins.

"I just spoke to a kid inside the grocery store. What's this about some notches on your knife?" Murphy asked.

"So the news is spreading fast, huh? I guess this is how reputations get started," Luca said, chuckling but not answering directly.

When Valerie and Luca finally reached the car, Valerie started to ask him about the story behind the notches. Just then, a call came in from the station. She spoke hurriedly, then, closing the phone, glanced over at him.

"A Navajo tribal officer delivered a package for you. It's at the downtown station."

He nodded. "Good. I'd like to pick it up as soon as possible. It's something I think you need—particularly when we speak to Navajo witnesses."

"What is it?"

"It's a very special *jish*—what some call a medicine pouch. When a Navajo sees that you honor our beliefs and are protected from the *chindi,* they'll be more inclined to speak to you."

"The *chindi?*"

"The good in a man merges with eternal harmony after death, but the evil side, the *chindi,* remains attached to this plane, waiting to create problems for the living." He paused, then in a slow, deliberate voice, continued. "Even though you don't share my beliefs, I wanted to protect you from a danger that is very real to me and those of my tribe."

Valerie had spent most of her life proving how tough she was. Maybe because of that, no one had ever said that they wanted to protect her. His concern filled her with a warmth that soothed her soul, softening all the hard edges she'd kept firmly in place all these years.

Suddenly horrified by her response to him, she mentally shifted gears. "By the way, what was that thing about the notches? Looks like a saw blade, kinda."

"Maybe I should just let your imagination come up with an answer," he said with a teasing grin.

"Let me guess. You're either a serial killer, or you like keeping track of the number of catfish you've gutted."

He laughed. "Those weren't notches. They're teeth for sawing wood. My dagger's a customized British commando knife."

"You really had all of us going with that," she said, laughing. "Remind me never to play poker with you."

After they stopped at the station, Luca picked up a small box from the desk sergeant while she went to check her computer. Afterward, armed with Mae Nez's address, they returned to the sedan, which was parked in an emergency vehicle space.

Once they were alone inside the unmarked cruiser, Luca slit open the box with a pocketknife and extracted the small, beaded leather pouch. "The contents of this *jish* are an extremely powerful, ancient form of protection. My father made this especially for you because, sometimes, the enemy you know least about is the one who poses the greatest threat."

Even knowing that she didn't share his beliefs, he'd cared enough to have this done. The gesture touched her deeply. "Thank you, and know that I'll have your back all the way, just as you've covered mine." She fastened the *jish* to her belt in the same way he wore his.

AS THEY DROVE AWAY from the station, silence settled between them. In that quiet, Luca became acutely aware of everything about Valerie. There was no doubt that she was a tough police officer, but he'd also caught glimpses of the gentle, feminine woman that lay within that strength. Fire and desire danced in her eyes when she looked at him, and that knowledge pounded through him, heating his blood. Sex was an appetite, and like hunger, it could be quickly and easily satisfied. Yet something warned him that taking her once would never be enough for him.

She was vastly different from Merilyn, the woman he'd intended to make his wife until fate had stepped in. Yet it was Valerie's independent streak and that mixture of toughness and vulnerability that called to him. She was exciting to be with, challenging on almost every level. And that was the problem. He'd never run from a challenge in his life.

As the radio dispatcher called and she reported their location, Luca led his thoughts back down a more disciplined track. Caring held dangers he wanted no part of. Everything had two sides. Even the innocent yucca plant that had brought Man and Woman together had given birth to another, much darker emotion—jealousy.

"Do you enjoy police work?" he asked, focusing on a much safer topic.

"Law enforcement is the only work that ever called me. It's what I was born to do," she answered, sounding completely at ease talking about something she obviously loved. "It demands everything and it's often round-the-clock, but I love it."

"Our jobs don't leave much time for a private life. Does that ever get to you?"

"I don't live the kind of life most women would choose for themselves, that's true enough. But most of my friends are in law enforcement, too, and understand the demands of my schedule. When I do have time off, I tend to spend it catching up on things I've left undone—like unpacking," she added with a grin. "It's a crazy lifestyle, but it suits me."

Something in Valerie's tone had spoken louder than her

words. Even as she'd justified the long hours, he'd sensed her leaving something out.

When Merilyn had died, he'd kept to an unbelievably punishing schedule filled with Brotherhood business and police work. He hadn't wanted time to think. The frantic pace—one similar to hers—had kept him from dwelling on things he couldn't change.

As he glanced at Valerie he wondered what she was running from. He had a feeling it was from herself, but he had no idea why she'd feel the need to do that.

"So what's life like for you on the Navajo Nation—the Rez, as you put it? Do cases come few and far between, or are they back-to-back like they are here?" she asked.

"With a much lower population density, I sometimes spend more time traveling than I do actually investigating. That means working long hours. But I take time for myself, too. That way I continue to walk in beauty."

"You've mentioned that a couple of times since we met. What exactly does that mean?"

"A good Navajo's life is defined by balance and order. When you're in harmony with all the different aspects of your life, you can walk in beauty."

"So now that you've seen how much order there is in my apartment, I guess I'm your worst nightmare," she teased.

"I could teach you a few things about the Navajo Way…." he said with a slow, thoroughly masculine grin.

The power of that gesture ribboned around her, squeezing the air from her lungs. She looked away, hoping she was wrong and she wasn't actually blushing.

Valerie cleared her throat then spoke. "Mae Nez's home is a good forty minutes out. We'll stop by her place of work first since it's closer. If she's not there, then we'll go to her house."

"Good plan."

"On the way there, make sure you help me keep an eye out for a tail, too," she said.

He nodded. "Considering I'm the enemy he challenged,

the killer is bound to start keeping close tabs on us." Realizing that his statement would lead to questions about the Brotherhood, he quickly added, "I'm the son of the tribe's most respected *hataalii,* so I'm undoubtedly in his sights. Since the snake didn't work, he's sure to try again."

As she remembered him shirtless, barely in his jeans, she sighed softly. He was magnificent to look at, easy to be with and intelligent. The whole package practically made her weak at the knees.

"What did your background search tell you about Mae?" he asked.

"Not much. She has no record. She's a student—part-time—and lives with her father." Valerie glanced over at him. "What's on your mind?"

"It's not likely that she's a Traditionalist, but her father may be. If we end up at her home, why don't you let me take the lead? By approaching them in a certain way, we may get further."

"You've got it." She knew that he wasn't just trying to take over. His focus was on the case and that was as it should be. They were detectives on the job. Nothing else should matter now. Yet it did…. Somehow she had to stop wondering how it would feel to lay against his chest and feel his arms around her.

"You're usually not this quiet. What's on your mind?" he asked.

She scrambled for a suitable answer. "This case—it's different from anything I've ever handled on almost every single imaginable level."

"It'll test each of us, and we may end up with a few more scars, but we'll find the answers we need."

Fighting the temptation to search for a hidden meaning in his words, she disciplined her thoughts and focused on the road.

Chapter Nine

They drove east up I-40 toward the community of Tijeras, nestled in the mountain pass between the Sandia and Manzano Mountains. Valerie remained quiet—mostly to prove she could—and Luca studied the crime reports and area maps, working while she drove.

After ten minutes with only a random radio call to mar the silence, she was ready to scream. "Okay, I give up. You win," she said at last.

He looked at her in surprise. "What are we playing?"

"Strong silent type—and I lose," she said with a martyred sigh. "Conversation doesn't always have a purpose, but considering we're still ten or more minutes from our destination, let's talk. It'll make the drive more interesting, too."

He looked at her and waited.

"Okay, then. I'll start," Valerie said. "You don't have a ring on, but I can't imagine a guy like you being completely unattached…."

"I am."

She immediately picked up on the change in his voice. "But you haven't been for long…."

He took a deep breath then let it out slowly. "She died in an accident a little over a year ago."

"Wife?"

"No, but she would have been."

"I'm so sorry," she said. The fact that he'd said "over a year" instead of giving her an exact number of months meant that he was past the worst of it. But some of the pain was still there…or maybe it was only the memory of that pain that lingered.

"And you?" Luca asked. "You're an outgoing, attractive woman. It's hard to believe that there's no one special in your life."

"I've dated mostly police officers over the years, but the truth is I like my freedom and independence. In law enforcement I have a gazillion rules I have to follow day in and day out. After hours I don't want to answer to anyone."

He smiled. "That feeling will pass when you meet the right person, and new priorities will take its place."

"Is that what happened with you?"

"Yeah. The right person changes your perspective—your whole outlook on life, actually. But I'm having a problem believing you've *never* met anyone who was special to you."

"Oh well, if you want to go back far enough there was one. Carlos and I were inseparable."

"What happened?"

"I outgrew the need for teddy bears."

He smiled. "Diverting away from the issue usually means you've got something to hide."

"I didn't duck it. I told you the truth. I've dated over the years, but things usually fall apart after a few months. One guy said I was 'emotionally unavailable,' whatever that means. What it all comes down to is that my job makes a lot of demands."

"No regrets?" he pressed.

"No, not really." Not until yesterday when Luca had stepped into her life. More than anything, she wished she could have met him under different circumstances. Mystery surrounded him and that constantly teased her imagination.

As they drove into the canyon, she took the exit south, passing through the intersection of old Route 66. It took another fifteen minutes before they found the place where Mae Nez worked, which was actually several hundred yards north of the interstate and around a big curve in the road. Valerie parked in front of the Sandzano Food Mart, noting that business at the small store wasn't exactly brisk.

As they came through the open door, a bell atop the entrance rang and an Anglo man behind the counter greeted them with a smile. "Hi there. Can I help you?"

Making sure that her badge was clearly displayed, she identified herself then added, "We're looking for Mae Nez."

"Is she in trouble?" the man asked quickly, giving them a worried look. "I'm Mike Smith. I own this place."

"No, not at all. We just need to ask Mae a few questions," Valerie answered, seeing four photos of employees on the wall behind the cash register. Only first names were listed below the photos, but one was Mae, who was wearing a store apron and sporting a shy smile.

Mike followed her gaze and nodded slowly. "That's Mae. I guess you want to talk to her about her friend's murder. Unfortunately, she's not here, and may not be home either. She asked for a few days off so she could go to the Rez and have a Sing done. Something that'll give her immunity from the ghosts of the dead." He looked at Luca, then added, "If you're Navajo, you're bound to know more about that than I do."

"The Sing is called Enemy Way," he responded, still looking at Mae's photo.

"Yeah, that's it," he said.

"Can you give us directions to her house?" Valerie asked, suspecting that the GPS wouldn't be much help.

Mike gave them directions then drew a map for them. "It's a hard place to find." He paused, then added, "There's a spring that flows through the area, and I understand there's been quite a bit of rain over there recently. If the creek's full, that homemade bridge of theirs might be a little risky. I suggest you park your car and go in the rest of the way on foot."

"Okay, thanks."

As they walked back outside, she glanced at the map and shook her head. "I guess we should have brought one of the department's four-wheel drive units. I hate to spend time walking unless it's part of the investigation."

He said nothing, his gaze taking in the area around them, especially the road leading back south toward the main highway.

Valerie glanced over at him and, accurately gauging his silence, added, "What's wrong?"

"Just a feeling—a bad one," he answered quietly, now looking farther ahead, north. "Stay on your guard."

"Cop's intuition?"

"A feeling," he said. "My father would call it '*álíl*—a power that doesn't lend itself to explanation."

"Do you think we're in immediate danger?"

He considered for a moment before answering. "No, but the danger's not far," he said, his voice quiet and too controlled to pass as natural.

"So we'll be just fine—till we're not," she commented with a rueful smile as they climbed back into the car.

"Don't say things like that. You need to guard your speech, particularly now. Your *jish* contains a crystal," Luca said, then explained, "Our ways teach that at the time of creation, a crystal was placed in the mouth of The People to make the spoken word come true."

"So I shouldn't say anything that I don't want coming true," she said, considering what he'd said. "Okay, I'll be more careful from now on." She paused thoughtfully for a moment before continuing. "Your ceremonies give you confidence to face whatever comes your way, don't they?"

"They restore the rightful balance of things and knowing that gives us power over fear," he answered.

"Your tribe—your beliefs—make you a part of something that can never be taken away from you. I envy you that."

"A Navajo is never alone, that's true. We have our ways, our clans, our tribe," he said. "Out here…it's very different."

"Remaining alone can make you strong, too," she said, for her own benefit as much as his.

Yet, despite her brave words, she knew Luca had awakened

a side of her she'd almost forgotten existed—the one that compelled a woman to find a mate.

Valerie instantly pushed that thought aside with every shred of willpower she possessed. Some doors were better left unopened.

"If you pick up on anything, or anyone, we need to be concerned about, let me know instantly," she said, her voice brisk and businesslike. "We can't get backup here inside a half hour, so we're on our own."

"He's out there," he answered softly.

"Somewhere in the county, New Mexico, the world? Or do you mean right behind us?" Valerie pressed, annoyed with him—and herself.

"Not directly behind us, no, but I can feel his presence," he said, then after a brief silence added, "He may have figured out where we're going and is already a few steps ahead of us."

"If you spot whoever's out there, catching him will become our first priority. The Nezes can wait."

"Agreed."

They drove south, crossing into the foothills of the Manzanos, the southern half of the spine of mountains that bordered the east side of the Rio Grande Valley. Soon they reached the turnoff, revealed by the rural mailbox with a number and the name *Nez* painted on its side.

The road was graveled, quite good for about a mile as it wound up into the juniper and piñon trees. At a fence line, though, it forked, and the route they took now was not much better than two deep tire ruts. After about a hundred yards, the ruts got so deep the car high-centered with a loud scrape and Valerie stopped.

Looking ahead, she cursed softly. "I'm not risking losing an oil pan just to save a few more steps. How about we walk from here?"

"Good idea," Luca said, opening his door. He climbed out slowly, looking around and listening but not moving away from the vehicle.

She checked her pistol, and with one last look in the rearview mirror, opened her door and joined him. "Let's find an easier route than that washboard of a road, but keep an eye out for the bridge Smith told us about."

"Someone else made the same decision. There's a trail that probably joins up with the road somewhere ahead."

"Trail?" She glanced around. "Where?"

"Look at the footprints leading down into that dry arroyo," he said, pointing Navajo-style.

She followed him down the incline into a steep arroyo. The sand at the bottom was just damp enough to make the footing solid rather than mushy, a good thing as far as she was concerned.

"There's the bridge," he said, after they'd walked about a quarter of a mile up a long slope.

The private bridge was made of logs and big square timbers, but the four supporting posts in the center of the structure had been knocked out of line by debris.

"Looks like the Nez family prefers to ford the channel," he said, pointing at the vehicle tracks leading in and out of the wash. "But the bridge should be safe enough for two people to cross."

She glanced at the rushing water below. It was probably not very deep but it was so muddy you couldn't really tell. If they waded across, one deep hole would be one too many for her today. "I choose the bridge."

"Keep an eye out as we work our way among the rocks. Snakes like to hole up during the day," he said, leading the way along the bank toward the old structure.

"Thanks for that wonderful reminder," she muttered sourly. Her boots were heavy and she was glad she'd worn them. It would be tough for anything that slithered to bite through them.

"When we get there, be sure to let the Nezes see your medicine bundle," he said. "And remember to avoid mentioning the dead by name. Doing that is said to call their *chindi*."

"I'll tell you what. You do all the talking. When I'm questioning a witness, I often lock on my goal and forget the rest.

I get answers, mind you, but your way is more…peaceful," she said with a tiny smile.

"That cost you," he said after a beat.

Valerie glared at him, but after seeing the playful gleam in his eye she burst out laughing. "You have no idea."

As she worked her way through the forest, branches from the pines and junipers beside the erosion-widened creek bed scratched her arms, making her skin itch. Small clouds of insects buzzed around her face. "I hate the woods. Give me streets, sidewalks, stoplights—and hot dog vendors."

"How can you say that?" he asked, genuinely surprised. "There's harmony out here. Nature even supplies you with signals that'll protect you from danger. The city can't compete with that."

"You've got to be kidding," she said, then stumbled on a rock that rolled beneath her boot.

Luca instantly reached out, circling his arm around her waist, and pulled her back against him, steadying her. "Listen," he whispered.

"To what?" Her heart was pounding in her throat. His body was pressed intimately against her from behind and she was exquisitely aware of everything about him—the hardness of his chest, the beat of his heart and the strength of his arm so gently wrapped around her.

"Danger," he said, his lips brushing her neck. "Play along."

"What's up, partner?" Valerie whispered, turning in his arms and brushing her lips against the base of his neck. Feeling him shudder made her feel wonderfully feminine and powerful.

"There's an armed man in the bushes to my left, about ten o'clock," he whispered. "When I say go, dive to your right and roll." He waited a second for his warning to sink in. "Go!"

Intending on blocking any shot with his own body, Luca dived in her direction, but Valerie had reacted a second faster than he'd planned. She was slightly ahead of him, in midair, when the shotgun went off. He heard the thump of pellets impacting into her just before they hit the ground.

Luca rolled right, yanked out his handgun and fired two quick shots as the shooter fled, crashing through the brush.

A blinding fear gripped him as he heard her groan. Instantly he scrambled over to where she lay. "Where are you hit?"

"Not hit…just knocked the wind out of me," she managed, struggling to catch her breath. "Get him."

Reassured, he jumped up and raced after the shooter.

Valerie sat up slowly. Her left ribs were throbbing, and it felt as if she'd been kicked by a mule. The ballistic vest had stopped the buckshot from penetrating but she'd be bruised for sure.

She'd barely made it to her feet when Luca returned, empty-handed.

"He's long gone," he said. "I heard a vehicle starting up farther down the road. How are you doing?"

"Thanking the powers that be that I was wearing a vest. But tell me something. *Why* did you dive in the same direction I did? Splitting up would have confused the shooter," Valerie pointed out.

Luca knew combat tactics, but didn't quite know how to explain his instinct to protect her. Knowing his decision was likely to annoy rather than flatter Valerie he started to plead momentary stupidity when a sound suddenly distracted both of them.

Luca and Valerie turned, pistols out and at the ready.

"Relax, guys, it's just me." Steve Browning came out from behind some bushes, camera in hand. "I've got a great photo of you two flying through the air." He looked at the back of his camera, studying the LCD display.

"You bozo!" Valerie yelled, putting her weapon away with a painful grimace. "We could have shot you!"

Luca bent down, picking up the spent brass from the two rounds he'd fired. "Did you get the shooter in the picture?" he asked as he stood.

"I didn't see him until you two dived for cover, so I just got him from behind. He was moving by then, too, so I doubt it'll be in focus."

Luca stepped up beside Browning, looking at the images on the digital display as the man scrolled though the shots he'd taken. All Browning had caught was the vague outline of a man wearing a green stocking çap and aiming a long weapon.

"I only had a second before he dived out of the frame," Browning explained as Luca stepped away again.

"How did you find us?" Valerie demanded.

"Your radio calls. I monitor police bands and you weren't using any of the tactical channels. It was easy."

She rolled her eyes. "Unless you want to end up in a fancy box six feet under, you better start rethinking what you're doing, Browning."

He looked down at her vest as she opened her jacket. "I saw the dust fly and assumed he'd missed, but you really did take a hit," he said, squeezing the shutter as he took another shot.

"Do that again and I'll be the one shooting," Valerie snapped. Digging into the vest fabric with her fingertips, she pulled out several rounds of buckshot and something else she didn't recognize. "What's this stuff?" she muttered, staring at the chunks of white material.

"That looks like skinwalker ammo," Browning said, coming closer. "They like shooting pieces of bone into you."

"Most of this is buckshot though," Valerie said, picking three more steel pellets out then placing the white fragments and rounds in an evidence bag.

"How did you know about bone ammunition?" Luca asked him.

"Internet."

"Listen to me carefully, Browning," Valerie managed through clenched teeth. "If you keep tailing us, I'm going to throw your butt in jail for interfering with an officer. Not that you'll thank me, but it might end up saving your life."

"You can't keep me from following, I know my rights as a member of the press."

"You're on shaky ground since you're not officially on

anyone's payroll and, believe me, I can make your life miserable," she said, holding his gaze.

"Sorry, Detective Jonas, but I'm going to be sticking to you like glue."

She hurt all over and was in a particularly foul mood because of it. Valerie took a step closer to the reporter, wanting to make him squirm.

Luca stepped in front of her, blocking the way, and faced Browning. "Evil ones don't like being brought out into the open. They thrive on secrecy and gain power from fear. You need to watch yourself. Your articles are making him front-page news and, like it is with police informants, that could easily turn you into the killer's next target."

"Maybe I better wear a bulletproof vest," Browning said slowly.

"Bullets are only part of what you should fear. Before anything happens, you'll see signs that'll let you know you've been targeted."

"You mean he'll warn me? How?" Browning asked quickly.

"Sometimes the evil one will slip a black rock into something you wear, a pocket, a saddlebag, a shoe even. Or maybe something you carry with you. Then your luck will start to change—for the worse."

"Something *I* carry or wear?" he repeated, then immediately searched his camera bag. "Nothing there," he said with a sigh of relief.

"You might also want to search your pockets," Luca said.

He reached inside his shirt and jeans front pockets. "Nada. Maybe he doesn't consider me a threat," he said. As he reached into one of his back pockets, he suddenly froze.

"What?" Valerie asked, now interested.

Browning slowly pulled his hand out of his left rear pants pocket. Nestled in his palm was a small black rock. "Okaaay…. I'll use this as part of my story," he said slowly, his voice wavering slightly despite an obvious attempt at confidence.

She was about to comment when she saw Luca glance at her and shake his head imperceptibly.

"Man, welcome to the world of *really* bad luck," Luca said in a somber tone. "You don't have protective medicine like us, which means you're about to get your first taste of an evil one's power. I'll be real surprised if the paper even buys your next article. Unless you take appropriate steps fast, your life is about to take one long nosedive into the pits."

"What can I do?" Browning asked.

"First of all, put as much distance as you can between yourself and the evil one," Luca answered.

Browning shook his head. "I can't do that. But what the heck. I don't believe in this stuff anyway. It's just superstition for simple…" Browning stopped in midsentence, cleared his throat and avoided eye contact with Luca. Turning aside, he brought out a small notebook and glanced at his notes, then added a few quick sentences.

"Talk to me a week from now," Luca said, silently noting the circle of fire sign of the Brotherhood sketched in pencil on the small pages along with other esoteric symbols of skin-walker magic. "And, by the way, you might want to search your car," he added.

"For what?"

"Anything and everything. It's a big part of your possessions and since you depend on it to make a living…" He shrugged.

Browning's eyes grew large. "I guess I better be on my way. Nothing more is likely to happen here today."

As Browning jogged back down the road, Luca chuckled softly then looked at Valerie. "I picked up that black rock at the same time I retrieved my spent brass. Then I dropped it into his back pocket while I was looking over his shoulder at the photos. I was trying to think of a way to keep him in line."

She laughed. "Good plan."

"But I'm still curious about his sources. I know he said the Internet, but the drawings I saw in his notebook…" He shook his head. "No way he got those there. They aren't that well known."

"What kind of drawings?"

"Some were like the ones found at the crime scenes, but the others—there's no way he should have known about them," he added, not mentioning the Brotherhood.

"Even if I push Browning to the wall, that guy's not going to reveal his sources, not if he ever expects to repair his career," she said. "But, in time, we might be able to find out some other way."

While Luca checked out the area where the shooter had made the attack, Valerie called in the incident using her cell phone. When she was finished, she walked over to where he was standing, still looking at the footprints of the shooter.

"Some kind of running shoes," he said. "I made a sketch, but you might want to take a couple of photos if your cell phone has one of those cameras."

"Yours does, too. Watch and I'll show you how it works." She brought out the cell phone and took two close-up shots, checking the quality. Standing up with a groan, she looked over. "Did you find an ejected shell?"

"I looked but there's no sign of one. I doubt he had time to pick it up, so I'm guessing it wasn't an autoloader. Probably a pump."

"And the BBs will be impossible to trace to a particular weapon. I've been meaning to ask. You must have heard the shooter when he came up. But how did you know where he was hiding?"

"It's like I told you. Everything out here speaks to those who know how to listen. The wind was blowing from east to west, but the leaves of the willow he was hiding behind were leaning to the north. I never heard him, but when I looked closely I saw the outline of the man—and what looked like a shotgun barrel."

"In the city we study people and learn how to read them. But plants?" She stretched, then winced.

Luca stepped to her side, placing his hand gently on her shoulder. "Let's go back to the city so you can have a doctor check you over. You could have a broken rib. We can always talk to the witnesses another time."

"No. I'm fine, just sore. We may have to walk slower than usual, but let's finish what we started."

"All right," he said, realizing from her tone that arguing the point would get him nowhere. "Once we get back, I may be able to help you get rid of the lingering pain caused by that punch to your chest."

"What did you have in mind?" she asked cautiously. He'd seemed serious about it, but her imagination had suddenly gone into hyperdrive. She could think of all kinds of wonderful ways for him to make her forget about the pain….

"Certain herbs and salves can help," he said. Giving her a slow smile, he added, "But there are other ancient ways, too, that might be even more effective."

Her mouth went dry and her heart began hammering. Although she knew the danger—Luca was definitely the "look but don't touch type"—it was like walking away from a particularly luscious, hot chocolate chip cookie. She'd never been good at resisting temptation.

Valerie was still considering his offer when they both heard rapid footsteps drawing near. Valerie and Luca reached for their weapons at the same time.

Chapter Ten

A second later an elderly Navajo man came down the path they'd been following. He was holding a shotgun, an old single-shot, but the barrel was pointed at the ground.

"Were you the ones who fired?" he demanded. "Hunting is illegal for another month, and this is no place for target practice," he said, noting the pistols at their waists.

"We're lawmen, Uncle. Someone took a shot at us but he got away," Luca said, then introduced himself in the old way. "We've come to speak to a Navajo woman who lives in this area. Her Anglo name is Mae Nez."

He nodded. "I'm known as Joseph Keeswood," he said, further identifying himself by his clans. "The one you're searching for is my neighbor's daughter, Nephew," he said. He glanced down at Luca's medicine bundle. "I know who you are—and who your father is. I've also heard stories from my relatives about the evil one that's been at work on the other side of the mountains. You were well chosen for this," he said with an approving nod. "Let me take you to the one you came to find. Her home's not far."

They crossed the old bridge, then walked southwest along an established path. They climbed into an area of transition between forest zones and began to encounter tall, long-needled ponderosa pines.

After about ten minutes, he stopped at the end of a stand

of pines and waved them ahead. "They live in the house across the meadow. Good luck to you, Nephew."

Luca and Valerie continued toward the home, and as they drew near they saw an elderly Navajo man and young woman packing suitcases into an old truck. Mae—whom they recognized from her photo—was dressed in Traditional clothes.

Luca stopped at the edge of the flower-covered meadow, motioning for her to do the same.

"They already saw us," Valerie said. "Why are we standing here?"

"We need to be invited to approach. If you go right up to them now, you'll get absolutely nothing useful from either of them," Luca said. "Look at the way the woman's dressed with that long, dark blue skirt and the loose-fitting blouse tied at the waist with a concha belt. And her hair is done up old-style in that bun. They're Traditionalists. I'd assumed she'd be a Modernist because she was a student, but maybe fear caused her to switch back to the old ways."

They waited in the hot sun for a full five minutes—an eternity by Valerie's standards.

Finally the short, stocky young woman waved, motioning for them to approach. *"Yáat'ééh,"* she said.

Luca introduced himself, naming his clans, then continued, "We need to speak to you about your friend."

"In that case, it's good you brought protection," Mae whispered, glancing down at their medicine bundles. "Bad things are happening here, Uncle. We woke up this morning and found an ash painting over by our truck. That's how it started for my friend, too. But what happened to her isn't going to happen to me."

Luca nodded slowly. "So you're leaving?"

"I was planning to go alone to my aunt's and having a Sing done, but that dry painting changes everything. My dad and I are going to the Rez and staying there until things settle down again."

"Tell me more about your friend. Why do you think she made such an enemy?" Luca asked.

Mae watched her father continue to load the truck for several seconds then answered. "I honestly don't know. The whole thing makes no sense to me. She wasn't even interested in our culture. The only reason she was taking Dr. Becenti's class is because she needed some credit hours in anthropology."

"I understand that she wanted to drop that class."

Mae nodded. "She made a low grade on her first term paper and got worried about losing her scholarship. Dr. Becenti offered to give her extra-credit work, but she really wanted to get out of his class. Dr. Becenti told her that it was too late but that he'd find a way to help her pass."

"And how did she take that?" Luca asked.

"My friend liked getting her own way. When Becenti didn't play ball, she went to the head of the department, Dr. Finley, and asked him for help. Finley told her that he couldn't interfere with another professor's grading, but that he would speak to Dr. Becenti on her behalf. That started a huge mess."

"What happened?" Valerie asked.

"Dr. Becenti was furious when he found out she'd gone to Dr. Finley. Those two really hate each other," Mae replied.

"What's the source of trouble between them?" Luca asked.

"Word has it that it's because of what happened last year. Dr. Finley got a lot of recognition from the tribe and the college for his journal article on Navajo healing rituals. Dr. Becenti, an expert on Navajo culture who'd been scheduled to research some secret society on the Rez—something that I heard would have completely upstaged Dr. Finley—got stonewalled by the tribe. I think his previous research into skinwalkers made a lot of people nervous, but I'm not sure about that. All I can tell you is that he wasn't able to finish his article and had to return all his funding. It was an embarrassing mess for the entire department. What made it *really* bad is that Becenti's part Navajo. Finley's Anglo, yet he not only got published, he was given some kind of award."

"When your friend got the dry painting, did she ask either professor about it?" Valerie asked.

"She went to Dr. Becenti. Since he's part Navajo she figured he'd know more about stuff like that. Besides, she didn't want to diss him because she still had to pass his class."

"So she snapped a photo and took it to him?" Valerie asked.

"With her cell phone, yeah. Then she rubbed it out with a stick," Mae said and shuddered. "My friend told me later that the photo really shook Becenti up. He warned her to watch her back and not go anywhere alone if she could help it. He even offered to teach her how to protect herself from things like that."

"Did she take him up on his offer?" Luca asked.

"Between school and her job, there wasn't time left over for anything else, but Dr. Becenti knew that and offered to meet her whenever she could get away. He really went the extra mile for her. A few times he drove her to the print shop where she worked so they could talk on the way."

"Do you think Dr. Becenti might have been attracted to your friend?" Luca asked.

"I don't know. All I can tell you is that he took time to help her even though she'd created problems between him and Finley. But even if Dr. Becenti had been attracted to her, it wouldn't have done him any good. She wasn't ready for another relationship—not after the way her last one ended."

"Tell us about that," Luca said, his attention focused on Mae, though in accordance with Traditional customs, he didn't make direct eye contact.

"She met Frank Willie, a member of our tribe, after she graduated from high school. He was a part-time student at the university. They moved in together for a while, but after several months things began to fall apart between them and she moved out. She told me later that Frank was just crazy and that it was time for her to focus on her own future."

"Did he ever get violent with her?" Luca asked.

"I don't know. If he did, she never said, and she never showed up with bruises or anything like that. Then again, that was during a time we didn't see each other that much."

"Do you happen to know where Frank lives now?" Valerie asked.

"No, but I think he's still a student at UNM, or at least he was last year. I saw him once or twice on campus," she said. "I didn't say hi or anything. Frank always creeped me out."

"Why? What about him made you uneasy?" Luca probed.

"He always kept secrets from my friend, and would go off for days without telling her. She'd get worried that something had happened to him, but if she said anything about it after he came back, he'd just get mad."

Seeing her father waving at her, Mae waved back. "I have to go now. I wish I could do more to help you catch the one who…" Tears formed in her eyes and she turned away.

"Is there a phone number where you can be reached if we need to talk to you again?" Valerie asked.

Mae nodded. "My aunt's," she said, giving Valerie the number.

After thanking her, Valerie and Luca walked back down the route they'd come. As the silence between them stretched Valerie considered the details of the case.

"Even though neither professor has a clear alibi according to the officer's report in my in-box, the issues between Becenti and Finley don't necessarily lead back to Lea in any clear way. But being dumped—that provides a motive for this Frank Willie character," she said. After a thoughtful pause she continued, "But if Willie's our man, why didn't he just kill Lea outright? Why bother with all the ritualism? And why attack the *other* girl? She wasn't even Navajo."

"She may have been a mistake, or maybe she knew Willie, too. We know that the two victims lived in the same area of the valley. I studied the map and they were practically walking distance from each other. We should track down Frank Willie as soon as possible, particularly because the rituals followed at each scene tend to indicate that the killer's Navajo."

Valerie nodded. "I agree, but it's still possible that Willie's not our man. If that's the case, we're back to square one and more people will die."

"The killer's taken great pains to do things like the ash paintings correctly—something another Navajo would notice," he said, thinking of the skinwalker's challenge to the Brotherhood. "That makes me think he prefers to focus on Navajo women, and that more from my tribe are in danger."

"Until we figure out how he chooses his victims, we won't know if he's after Navajo women and vic one was a mistake, or if he's looking for women who fit a certain description. Or it could be that he's after women who've offended him in some way—real or imagined—and it's just a coincidence they lived in the same area."

As she slipped behind the wheel, pain shot through her and she winced. Without much protest, she took Luca up on his offer to drive.

While en route back to the city, Valerie called the station, requesting a location on Frank Willie. A deputy was sent to his last known address, but by the time they reached the city, they'd learned that Willie had moved out weeks ago. At the moment, they had no idea where he might be living.

ONCE THEY REACHED home, Valerie was ready for a break. They went past the guard at the front desk, then directly upstairs. As soon as they were inside the apartment, Valerie dropped onto a chair. "Would you go into the bathroom and get me some pain reliever? There's some in the medicine cabinet," she said. "No, forget that. Bring me the whole bottle."

"I can make you feel better without that," he said.

"If you're going to make a pass at me, could you wait until I can at least pretend not to enjoy it?" she teased with a tired smile.

Standing before Valerie in his dark T-shirt and jeans, he

gazed at her. "There's a tub in the large bathroom and I have some herbs that'll do wonders for the soreness you feel. All you have to do is soak for a while and let their medicine take effect."

Luca stepped out of the room and the next thing she heard was the sound of the bathwater running. Valerie sighed, mildly disappointed that he hadn't made a pass at her after all. For a moment or two she considered making one herself.

Luca came back a moment later and, without asking, scooped her up in his arms and carried her to the bathroom. "Let me undress you. I won't take advantage," he murmured, not setting her down yet.

"Then I'd have to take advantage of you," she said, enjoying the way he'd wrapped his arms so securely and gently around her.

"Be careful," he growled. "You might find more than you're prepared to handle." He pressed his lips to her forehead and set her down.

His tenderness spiraled around her, softening his words of warning and turning them into a whisper of a promise, a hint of what could be.

His gaze slid down her body slowly and thoroughly, leaving her tingling everywhere. Then, wordlessly, he walked out and shut the door behind him.

Telling herself that it was a good thing he hadn't stayed, Valerie undressed. The bathroom was filled with the most wonderful scent of wildflowers. Stepping into the welcoming warmth of the tub, she lay back, closing her eyes, and a feeling of peace enveloped her.

As her thoughts drifted, she thought of Luca…a man like no other, the one who could make her believe in the power of magic.

SHE WASN'T SURE how much time had passed when she heard a knock at the door. "Captain Harris is on the line. He wants to speak to you," Luca said.

Struggling to become wide-awake, she wrapped a towel around herself then opened the door to take the phone from Luca.

"Detective Jonas," she said briskly.

"You didn't file a full report last night, Jonas. I need to know what progress you've made."

"I'm still on the case, Captain Harris," she said, updating him quickly. "I just needed to make a stop by the apartment to get a change of clothing."

"No explanation needed, Detective. You were attacked and hit. That buys you a few hours off," he said. "But I'm under pressure from above and I don't like having my butt hanging out in the wind. I need answers."

"Got it, Captain."

Luca took the phone from her hand. "You're bleeding," he said quietly.

Valerie saw the small, round spot of blood near the top of the white towel and turned toward the mirror above the sink.

"Let me lower the towel just a bit," he said, stepping closer. "You're okay," he said, as he revealed what was only a small scratch.

As his hand brushed the skin just above her breast, the gentle contact made her draw in her breath and a shiver coursed through her.

"Don't do that." He bit off the words, acutely aware of her reaction to him.

"Or you'll do what?" she whispered. His eyes had turned as black as midnight and she could feel the warmth of his breath touching her lips.

In an instant, he lifted her up, forcing her back against the tile wall and kissed her. His tongue danced intimately with hers while his hands drifted down to her hips, holding her steady against him.

Eternities went by before he broke the kiss and moved back, his gaze still on her. "Next time we'll both need more."

Before she could unscramble her brain enough to respond, Luca walked into the next room.

Valerie leaned back against the wall trying to even her breathing and wondering if her heart would ever stop racing. Luca was as unpredictable as the four elements—and, without a doubt, the most exciting man she'd ever met.

Chapter Eleven

She'd dressed and her insides had stopped thrumming by the time she entered the living room again. As she did, her cell phone rang.

"We've got something from the crime lab," Captain Harris told her. "The bones found at the first crime scene came from animals. The ones from the second are human in origin. Looks like he's turning it up a notch."

"Did the bones at the most recent scene come from the first victim?" Valerie asked.

"No. I think he's decided to hold on to the fingers he amputates as trophies. Are you ready for the really interesting part? The bones at crime scene number two are from someone who has been dead for at least forty years, maybe longer."

Valerie considered it. "So we're not talking an archaeological dig. Any established cemetery would fit the bill."

"More tests will be run on the bones. Maybe we can learn the sex and race of the person they belong to. And one more thing. We had the computer list comparisons between crimes and one interesting fact came up. Victim number two, Lea Begay, and vic one, Ernestine Ramirez, both walked down the same ditch bank on their way home each evening. That tends to indicate that the killer knew the habits of his victims. So the chances that they were selected at random appears far less likely now."

Valerie hung up and immediately filled Luca in. "So maybe vic one was a mistake, as you'd suggested. A similar-looking young woman came down the path close to the expected time and in the low light, he assumed it was his target."

"Or maybe it was just a practice run," Luca said. "But it leads to the same conclusion. The Navajo girl was his intended target."

"Killing her on the ditch bank was a lot more private than the backyard of a city neighborhood just two streets over from one of Albuquerque's busiest avenues. All things considered, I think the first girl was in the wrong place at the wrong time," Valerie said, going over to her laptop computer.

She accessed the department computer records and studied the facts uncovered by the crime scene teams. "The deputies who interviewed the students in victim number two's class have filed their reports. It's a small group, and most of the guys either had alibis for the time of death or were ruled out for other reasons. One, for example, was in a wheelchair."

"Anyone at the college, particularly in the anthropology department, could have had access to bones in some of the lab settings—but I assume they'd be much older than a few decades," Luca said.

"The logical place to find a supply of bones the age our perp is using is at a cemetery. We should find places that aren't in high-traffic areas, like the ones off Menaul Avenue or in Martineztown. Maybe he dug up a grave beside an old church in one of the outlying communities, like Corrales or Bernalillo. Assuming he's digging at night, chances are he wouldn't exactly run into masses of people."

He nodded. "Right. And if this is the same individual that the gang members almost collared at that neighborhood pet cemetery, he's being extra careful now. But even if he's gone human-grave robbing, that doesn't necessarily mean he's left a trail we can follow."

"Then let's narrow it down to just a few places and stake out the most likely ones." She paused abruptly, then quickly added, "I'll handle this part myself. I know about your beliefs and the *chindi*."

Luca shook his head. "I appreciate the offer, but this is why I carry safeguards that protect me. I know my responsibilities—and I don't run out on my partners." He stood rock still, unmovable, his gaze steady.

His answer didn't surprise her. This wasn't a man who ran—from anything. "Okay, then we'll start our survey during the daytime, see if any graves have been disturbed, then target the most likely ones for a return visit after nightfall."

As she began a computer search for old graveyards and burial grounds in and out of the county, she saw him walk to the far side of the room and open a backpack filled with Navajo articles, some familiar to her, some not.

Determined to give him privacy, Valerie concentrated on her work. Soon he began a soft Sing. Although she couldn't understand the words, there was something soothing about the monotone chant.

With effort, she kept her attention focused on the computer screen, and eventually narrowed down three sites based on locale. Two of them appeared to be good bets, located in old communities up on the east side of the Sandia Mountains, north of where they'd been earlier in the day and on forest service land. She ruled out the third once she saw it was situated beside a busy street.

Luca had finished the chant. Valerie glanced back at him as he was placing something in his pocket. "I know you were preparing for what we'll be doing next, but can you tell me more about what you did?" she asked.

He held out his hand and in the center of his palm was a small stone carving. The animal fetish was in the form of a cougar. Powder of some kind covered it.

"It's beautiful, but what's it mean?" she asked, noticing how the polished stone caught the light.

"A few years back, I investigated a case where a Zuni medicine man was accused of murder on the Navajo Nation.

He was innocent, and I was able to find evidence that cleared him and convicted the one really responsible. In gratitude, he carved this special fetish for me. It's made of flint, which is a very powerful mineral to my tribe. When the monsters that preyed on the earth were killed, their blood and hide turned to what we know today as flint. The flash of color and light it emits frightens away evil."

"But why a cougar?" she asked.

"Each fetish embodies the attributes and powers of the animal it represents. Those, in turn, become part of the human that feeds it. Corn pollen, the powder covering the fetish, stands for life and nourishes Cougar, keeping his power strong."

He grew silent for a moment and, unable to suppress her curiosity, she asked, "What special powers does Cougar have?"

"I was going to get to that," he said, then laughed.

That deep-bodied, masculine sound rippled over her like a shower of sparks. "Hey, I'm a curious girl."

"Curiosity is what makes you a good detective. Lack of patience…well, that one could work against you." He brushed her cheek with the palm of his hand then moved away.

The gentleness of his touch kindled a fire inside her, but she remained where she was, fighting the urge to draw closer to him. As the silence stretched out, Valerie knew he was testing her. Rather than press him, she went to the computer, shut it down and grabbed her jacket.

Luca followed her out. Once they were inside the quiet of the car, he finally answered her. "Cougar is known to be a resourceful hunter whose intelligence is matched by his strong will. Nothing ever stands in his way. Cougar sticks to his objective because giving up isn't part of his nature."

"The Zuni medicine man made a wise choice. Those attributes fit you like a second skin," she said. "It also supports a theory I've had about you—for why you became a detective."

He raised an eyebrow and waited.

She didn't answer right away, making him think about it

like he'd done to her. Yet, to her surprise, he didn't seem in the least bit perturbed by the silence.

Finally giving up, she spoke. "Police work called to you in a way nothing else could. Living life on the edge suited you perfectly. Your spirit wasn't meant to be stranded behind a desk. The rush you get from our type of work keeps your blood pumping. I'm right, aren't I?" She smiled, satisfied that her conclusions were correct.

Luca shook his head. "Not really. Though I suspect that's what drew you to the work, my reasons were different. I went into police work because I wanted to take an active role restoring the balance between good and evil. My father does that by serving as a *hataalii,* but a *hataalii* has to wait until his patients need him. In law enforcement, the hunt's always active and it's never ending. That's why I chose it."

She glanced over at Luca, then back at the road. Nothing about him was ordinary. He stood taller than most men in almost every way that mattered. He was exciting to be with…yet it was his stillness that drew her. Peace, the kind that seemed to be so much a part of him, was something she'd never known.

FORTY MINUTES LATER, they approached Holy Angels Cemetery. Locating the wooden rail fence that defined the grounds, Valerie drove down an old gravel lane leading off the highway and parked near the entrance.

As they left the car, they both heard a metallic clinking sound up ahead behind a stand of tall blue spruce. Since they were the only spruce trees within sight, it appeared that they'd been planted. Their height also suggested that it had been many years ago.

"It's a hoe," Luca said. "Someone's planting something, or maybe weeding."

All she'd heard was a chink, but then again she'd never weeded or planted anything in her life.

"There," he said a moment later, and gestured ahead, beyond the trees.

A man in his midseventies, clad in coveralls and an old straw hat, was busy planting flowers in a sunny spot beside a gravestone.

Valerie identified herself as she approached him.

"I'm Ed Black," he answered, taking off his hat and wiping the sweat from his brow. "What brings you two up here?"

"Have you noticed anything unusual going on at this cemetery within the past few weeks?" she asked.

He shook his head. "No, not really, but I'm not the caretaker, if that's what you think. I just happen to be the only one who ever comes out here. This cemetery's closed now, and no one takes care of the grounds—except me. I planted those trees back in '84, the year after my wife Heather died. Now, I cut the weeds when I can and keep her grave tended."

Valerie glanced around. Grass grew tall beside most of the graves. "It does seem pretty desolate out here."

"People tend to want to forget all about the dead. They don't like to be reminded that as we are, the person in the grave once was. And as those below the earth are now, we'll someday be."

Cheery thought, but accurate. "Have any of the graves here been disturbed in any way?" Valerie asked.

"Except for me trimming the grass a little and weeding around Heather's grave, no, not at all. This rocky mountain soil is just too hard except in spring, when the snow all melts. The old coffins, too, were sturdier," he said, brushing away a spiderweb from the side of the headstone.

Thanking the old man and leaving him to his work, they took a quick walk around the cemetery, but it was just as he'd said. Nothing appeared out of place.

"His wife died twenty-six years ago. I saw the date on the headstone. But even after all this time, he still comes here," Valerie commented softly.

"Grief can take you to some very dark places," Luca said after a long pause. "You can eventually work your way back, but you're never the same afterward."

Valerie started to ask him more, intrigued and wanting to know everything she could about him, but he shook his head. "It's behind me," he said in a tone that held nothing but finality.

As they reached the sedan, she glanced at the GPS mounted in her unit searching for the other cemetery she'd earmarked. It was east, farther down the mountain and close to one of the newer, developed communities with high-end homes. That area was undergoing a transformation and new roads were being added constantly. Making sure of the route, she began the drive.

"I sure hate to see older folks who appear to be all alone like that gentleman back at the cemetery. The only purpose his wife's death served was to blast a hole through his heart."

"On the face of things it might seem that way, but life needs its opposite—death. Together, they achieve balance."

"Then that design needs some work," Valerie muttered.

"We can't change the pattern, but by recognizing and accepting it, we walk in beauty," he said. "One of our creation stories explains the need for such things. Would you like to hear it?"

"Yes, please." The fact that he'd asked her first, honoring the possibility that her beliefs might not permit it, touched her deeply. That kind of respect—for himself and others—was very much a part of the man he was and why she was so drawn to him.

"When the Hero Twins of old defeated all the monsters that preyed on the earth, they thought their work was complete. But then they met four strangers—Cold, Hunger, Poverty and Death." His rich voice wove a spell around her, bringing the ancient story alive in her mind's eye.

"The Twins immediately decided to kill them, but Cold, who spoke first, told them that without him there'd be no more snow, or water in summer. So the Twins considered what he'd said and decided to let him live."

She nodded slowly and, careful not to interrupt, waited for him to continue.

"Then the Twins faced Hunger, who said that if they killed

him, people wouldn't take pleasure in eating anymore, and eventually everyone would lose their appetites. The Twins realized then that they had to let him live, too.

"Poverty was a filthy old man in dirty clothing. He told them that, without him, people would stop wanting and making new clothes and everyone would look as dirty and ragged as he did. So the Twins also spared him."

His voice mesmerized her. Scarcely breathing, she waited for him to finish.

"Then the Twins faced Death. She was a horrible creature, disgusting to look at. The Twins wanted to kill her immediately, and, to their surprise, she told them to go ahead. She didn't care. But she warned them that without her, the older generation would stop yielding to the younger. Young men would stop dreaming dreams that made for better tomorrows. They wouldn't marry, or have kids who'd someday take their place. She insisted that although it didn't seem to be so, she was their friend." He paused for a moment, then in a soft voice added, "And that's why we still have death."

"The Navajo Way is filled with such incredible beauty. It gives you a way to deal with the things that scare the pants off the rest of us," she said softly. "Of course, we have our own way of coping. We just tell ourselves that we're not really scared," she added with a tiny smile.

"Some of us inside this car excel at that, I would imagine," he teased, curving his mouth into one of his devastating smiles. "And since I don't fit the bill, that leaves you."

"Hey, I'm indestructible. I can outshoot and outfight almost any officer in the department—and when I'm scared, I fight all the harder," she said as they headed down the road.

"So I've noticed," he answered gently.

She glanced at him and knew instantly that he was talking about the attraction between them. She looked back at the road, not bothering to deny it.

Soon they reached the paved road and she turned onto the

highway. As they headed down the narrow mountain road, he touched her arm lightly.

"Slow down," he said. His voice was taut.

"I'm going the speed limit. Is something wrong?"

"The fetish...it shifted in the bag and it's pushing against me."

"Is that bad?" she asked quickly.

"It's a warning."

She let off the gas petal instantly. Whether or not she fully accepted his ways, one fact remained. His instincts had been right on target every time.

Preparing to slow down even more as they reached a curve, she touched the brakes. "Something's not right. The brakes feel spongy—and the brake light just came on."

Valerie pressed the brakes even harder but the car barely slowed, even when she pushed the brake pedal all the way down to the floor. "The brakes are completely gone! Hang on!"

Looking ahead, her stomach tightened. They'd never make that curve at their current speed. Valerie steered to the right, off the pavement and onto the narrow shoulder, hoping the gravel there would slow them down. The right front tire dropped over into the drainage ditch, and she had to fight for control as the car shifted violently. There was an ear-shattering *whack* as the branch of a tree whipped against the windshield.

"You're doing fine," he said calmly. "Good strategy. You've slowed us down already."

"I can't turn off the ignition or I'll lose steering. Let me try the parking brake."

Valerie lifted the lever with her right hand, applying pressure. It cut their speed even more, but it wasn't enough and it distracted her from keeping the car on track.

Edging over to the right, she eased the passenger-side tires off the road, bumping into debris that had slid down the mountainside. If they blew a tire that would bring them to semi-safe stop—*if* she could keep from losing complete control of the car.

"There's a firebreak ahead, just before the curve. Get as

much grab as you can from the hand brake, then go hard right and try to jump the ditch into the field. If we don't roll, we'll end up in the clearing between the lines of trees. The brush and the fact that it's uphill will eventually bring us to a stop."

"*If* the car doesn't roll," she repeated. Valerie edged to the right again. "I'm going to kiss the hillside one more time. Maybe that'll help. It'll scrape the hell out of your side of the car, so stay low in case the window breaks."

"I'd rather see it coming," he said, leaning toward the center to avoid the possibility of glass.

The screech of metal against rock and timber, like monster fingers on a chalkboard, sent chills up her spine. The car shook and shuddered like a wild carnival ride, but she kept her death grip on the wheel.

A hundred yards from the firebreak, Valerie applied the hand brake, then took hold of the wheel with both hands and swerved to the right. The tires squealed in protest at the sudden turn and for a heartbeat the passenger side lifted off the ground.

They flew over the low ditch, plowed through a clump of waist-high brush then bumped their heads on the inside roof as the wheels hit the ground again. They bounced and skidded another fifty yards uphill, then finally came to a stop in a tangle of scrub oaks. A cloud of dust passed over the car then quickly dissipated.

"You okay?" Valerie asked, still gripping the wheel. Her hands wouldn't uncurl.

"Yeah. Nice driving," he said, his voice calm as usual.

She took a deep steadying breath. With a shaky grin she asked, "Wanna do it again?"

Chapter Twelve

As they climbed out of the car, Luca was relieved to find that the cougar fetish had once again shifted in his pocket and had stopped pressing against him. He glanced over at Valerie and realized that despite her bravado, the ride had really shaken her up. She had her arms wrapped around herself, trying to stop trembling.

Without hesitation, he pulled her against him and held her, allowing her softness to melt into him. He'd intended to be tender, to simply hold her and comfort her, but needs slammed into him with surprising force. He took a slow, deep breath, struggling to keep himself in check.

"That was the wildest ride I've ever been on, but even though your heart's pounding, you're not even breathing hard," Valerie said, nestling against him with a sigh.

"Other things make me breathe hard."

As she laughed softly, he felt those vibrations touch every part of him. Valerie's strength was matched by her wild spirit. Instinct assured him that in his arms her wildness would lead them both to a paradise neither would ever forget. That sure knowledge pounded through him, heating his blood, making him want her all the more.

Moments later she moved away and gave him a shaky smile. "Now that we've proven we're both still alive," she said with a soft sigh, "I've got to call this in." She contacted the station with her cell phone as they walked back down toward the road.

Less than three minutes later they heard a car coming up the highway. "That's a fast response—unless a cruiser was nearby."

"Doesn't sound like a police car to me," Luca added, looking down the mountain.

A minute later an older model yellow sports car came around the curve and puffed up the road toward them. As the driver came to a halt they recognized him instantly.

"Browning," Luca said.

"That pain in the butt must have been tailing us again. Or maybe monitoring police calls," Valerie said.

"Hey, you guys get stuck or something?" Browning called out. Turning around quickly in the empty highway, he parked beside them, then climbed out of his vehicle. As he came toward them, he studied the skid marks and churned-up ground where they'd left the roadbed. "Whoa! You take a corner too fast and head off cross-country or something?"

"Or something," Valerie replied.

"Did you pass any other cars on the road when you came up?" Luca asked him.

"There was a white van that whipped past me a few minutes ago, but that's about it. So what happened to your car? You get run off the road? Have a blowout?" he pressed, looking uphill at the unmarked police unit.

"You never have a flat when you need one," Valerie responded, unwilling to give the man anything to work with.

Browning looked at her curiously, then brought a digital camera out of his jacket pocket and took a photo of the car. He reached for his small notepad next, but the second he began to write his felt-tip pen started to drip. A blob of black ink came out onto the paper, making an instant mess.

Browning looked at his blackened fingers and cursed, then noticed the bottom of his shirt pocket was spotted with ink as well. "I've had nothing but crappy luck since I found that cursed stone in my pocket."

"Perhaps you should back away from this case," Luca advised, his face revealing nothing. "It's for your own safety."

"No way. This story's going to get me back on the payroll. I'm not spending the rest of my life teaching," he said. Then, looking from one to the other, he added, "Does this have anything to do with that graveyard you checked out a while ago?"

Luca shrugged.

"I bet those bones at the crime scene were human and you're trying to find dug-up graves. Am I right?" Browning prodded.

"No comment. Thanks for stopping, your Good Samaritan obligation has been met for today. Let us walk you back to your car," Valerie said coldly.

They went with him over to his parked car and saw the long, deep scratch that ran the entire length of the passenger side of his car.

"What happened to your ride?" Valerie asked him. "Did you piss off some witness?"

"Nah, some idiot kid keyed my car last night outside the health-food store, can you believe it? I'm telling you—crappy luck. That's all I've been having."

Luca held his palms face up and shrugged in a gesture that plainly said, "I told you so."

"So, do you need a ride back to civilization?" Browning asked them.

Valerie shook her head. "No, we're waiting for a deputy."

"In that case, I'll be on my way," he said.

As he drove off, Luca walked back uphill toward their unit.

"What's on your mind?" she asked, following him through the grassy meadow.

"I know a few things about cars. I want to take a look at the brake line and cylinders," he said. "Brakes don't go from good to bad that quickly—not very often, anyway."

Luca disappeared under the car and a moment later called back to her. "It looks like one of the connections came loose and that resulted in a fatal loss of brake fluid—and stopping power. It was tampered with, I'm guessing, but this is beyond my expertise. The crime scene unit will have to work on this, and I'll be willing to bet that they'll need a mechanic looking over their shoulders, too."

The sound of another vehicle diverted their attention toward the highway. A deputy was climbing out of an unmarked unit.

As they walked over to join him, another marked police cruiser arrived. "I was told to bring you this car," the deputy said, tossing Valerie the keys. "Someone will stay with your car until it can be towed. A team's on its way, but dispatch didn't think you needed the mobile van."

"No, just some experts to check out the car before it's hauled away. Thanks," Valerie added, handing over the keys to her own vehicle. She then turned to Luca. "We've still got daylight. What do you say that we complete what we set out to do?"

"The cemetery?" he asked, following her to the car.

She nodded. "By the way, if you happen to sense danger again, just let me know," she said with a shaky smile, starting the engine and pulling out into the road. "I won't be so slow on the uptake next time."

The uneasiness he could hear in her voice felt like a weight on his shoulders. "Is it difficult for you to accept things that don't lend themselves to explanation?"

She considered it then nodded. "A bit. It's a combination of private skepticism and police training. I'm more comfortable with hard facts."

"Then rely on this—you can trust me. No matter what goes down, I'll be right there with you. You'll never have a better partner."

"Or a more dangerous one," she muttered.

Somehow, he managed to hear her. "Dangerous to others perhaps, but never to you."

Even as he spoke, he could feel her responding to him. What was drawing them together was nature at its most basic…and more. No woman had ever gotten under his skin like this, making him ache and wish for things he had no business wanting. Not even his beautiful Merilyn had exercised so much power over him.

Silence stretched out between them for several long minutes before she spoke, bringing their focus back to the business at hand. "The place where we're going next isn't exactly an official cemetery. Basically it's an area at the base of a hill where people have been buried for the last fifty years or so. That was well before the developers moved in."

"How did you find out about it?"

"I knew it was there already, so all I had to do was double-check. My mom and I lived in this area for a while. She and I moved around a lot, and one summer we worked at one of the tourist stops along the highway."

"What was it like for you back then?" Luca asked. Something about her tone had caught his attention. It had held sadness...and something more, maybe regret.

"Does the past matter? It was a long time ago," she said, taking a deep breath.

"We don't have to talk about it if it makes you uncomfortable," he said.

"It's not that. The thing is, I've spent a lot of time and effort creating a new life for myself and it seems pointless to go over old ground."

"Who you are today is the result of who you were back then—both the good and the bad," he said.

"How about a trade?" Valerie asked after a pause. "I answer your questions, then you answer mine. And nothing's off-limits."

He knew that she'd added that last part as a challenge, but he'd never backed off from a challenge in his life. "You've got yourself a deal."

"All right then," she said with a nod. Taking a breath, she continued. "My mom and I moved around a lot back then," she said, answering his question. "She was never happy staying put in one place for long. My mother spent her entire life searching for something that was always just out of her reach. In the process, we made our living as housekeepers, house sitters, pet sitters, store clerks, evening custodians—whatever jobs we could get. We weren't rich but, somehow, we always got by. One of the places we stayed at was near where we're going now. It belonged to a ski instructor my mom had a thing for and we worked in his shop. By then I was in high school, and the future was all I could think about. I'd already decided what I was going to do after UNM—go into the FBI."

"Why didn't you?"

"After thinking it over, I decided that I could make more of a difference here, in the area where I grew up. That's how I ended up with the Sheriff's Department," she said, slowing as they came upon an old pickup loaded with firewood.

"As a kid, did you like moving around so much?"

"That's your third question, buddy," Valerie said with a grin. "If I answer, that'll mean I get three, too. Do we have a deal?"

He nodded once.

"I *hated* moving—back then and even now. Too much of a hassle," she said. "But these days all I need is a place for my stuff. I'm more at home out on the streets, on the clock, wearing the badge."

Luca met her gaze, understanding far more than she'd intended to reveal. A part of her needed a home base, yet she was afraid of the side of her nature that yearned for things like that. It made her too vulnerable, and she'd seen too much of the world to welcome that feeling.

They reached the main highway, then drove farther north for about a mile before arriving at their destination. Valerie pulled off the road and parked where the trees were thin and the grasses tall.

Putting off her questions for now, she announced, "We'll have to go in on foot from here."

They hiked uphill for a quarter of a mile on the remnants of a rock- and flagstone-lined path, now mostly overgrown with weeds and the rare intrusion of a young juniper or two.

As the ground evened out somewhat, they found themselves at the bottom of a rocky slope filled with old stone markers. Some were finely carved with names and dates, others merely stacks of rocks that denoted a grave. There had been a stone wall around the cemetery at one time, but now it was mostly rubble that stood less than a foot high.

They walked around, trying to find evidence of shovel marks, replaced turf or traces of fresh dark earth aboveground. At a small knoll, Valerie stopped and looked downhill. "The view from here is always beautiful, no matter what time of year."

"Notice how lush the growth is against the mountainside," Luca commented, turning toward the cliff. "There must be a spring up in those rocks," Luca commented.

"Which reminds me—I'm thirsty. Let's get this search over with. I hear a can of soda calling me." She continued ahead, making her way across a stretch of uneven ground.

"The earth's very soft here," Luca said. "Look at the moss."

As she sidestepped to avoid a particularly muddy spot, Valerie lost her balance and fell sideways. Luca reached out to break her fall, but the ground suddenly gave way beneath both of them. They plummeted downward, breaking through a thin crust of soil into an underground air pocket.

They tumbled down several feet, then landed feetfirst in a clear stream of water less than two feet deep. The bottom of the pool was as hard as bedrock.

"This water's freezing," Valerie said, her teeth chattering. "What did we do, drop down into an old well?"

Luca saw human bones protruding out from the side of the hole in the direction the water was flowing. "This is a sinkhole formed beneath one of the graves. It looks like that spring I suspected was here has washed away some of the soil beneath the cemetery," he said, turning to look around the ten-foot-wide cavern. The hole they'd created up above provided enough light to see each other and the muddy sides of the opening.

As she touched the moisture-filled walls of the cave, Valerie knew there'd be no climbing back out. The sides were too slippery and wouldn't hold their weight, and the only roots sticking out were too small. She took her cell phone out but got no signal.

Valerie stared upward through the jagged skylight and the blue sky beyond. "Any suggestions?"

"Even if you stand on my shoulders, you still won't be able to reach the top," he said after a moment. "But there's light coming from the other end of the stream."

He pointed down at the icy water that flowed out from a hole about three feet wide. The rocks around the opening looked clean and polished, as if the flow had been running for centuries.

"That means there might be an opening in another chamber that leads back outside, right?"

"Exactly," he answered. "Here, hold my weapon. I'll go take a look."

Luca handed her all his gear, took a deep breath then ducked down under the water and swam under the ledge. A moment later he came back into view.

"There's another larger cavern tucked into the hillside up ahead. It may give us a way out—or at least lead us in the right direction." Luca rubbed his arms. "But brace yourself. That water's like ice."

"I'd rather freeze than just sit around waiting for help. Are there any more skeletons on that side?" she asked, glancing around. She wasn't Navajo, but this place would creep anyone out, and when it got dark…

"No, not there. Just a big, rocky cavern. It's drier than in here, but it smells funky."

"Thanks for the warning." She gave him his weapon back, then asked. "How are we going to keep our stuff dry? Wait—I've got some evidence bags in my pocket," she added, answering her own question.

Several minutes later, they were sitting on a big, cold rock inside the adjacent cavern. Valerie was shivering uncontrollably and Luca placed his arms around her, bringing her closer to him. He wanted to use his body to warm hers, but he was as cold as ice.

"We need heat," she managed through chattering teeth. Without hesitation, she followed her instincts and drew his mouth down to hers. She'd wanted heat, but what happened next went beyond all her expectations.

Cradling the back of her head, Luca parted her lips then slowly took possession of her, making her burn with desire. As his tongue caressed hers in a gentle dance, she felt herself melting into him. Intense longings she'd never experienced before filled her.

When he pulled back, taking a breath of air, she whimpered, unwilling to let it end so soon.

Luca held her gaze for a heart-stopping moment, then took her mouth again. The hardness of his kiss and the gentleness of his tongue sent fire coursing all through her. She wanted more, and gave more. Here in this darkness, in this hidden cavern of secrets, she was finding something she'd never dreamed existed.

When Luca at long last moved away, she felt more alone than she'd ever thought possible. She edged closer to him, wanting more of those exquisite sensations she'd found in his arms, but he suddenly signaled her to remain still.

Luca held a finger to his lips and took a step forward. "Did you hear that?" he whispered.

"What?" She looked at him in confusion. The only thing she'd heard was the thundering rhythm of her heart.

He held up one hand, and a second later she heard it, too. The scuffing sound suddenly stopped. She tensed and opened the sealed pouch that held her gun.

"No," he said in a barely audible voice.

Hearing a soft sound behind her, she turned her head. Relief flooded through her as she saw the animal that stepped into the chamber. "What a big, beautiful cat," she said, bending down and calling to him.

"Get up. That's no kitty," Luca warned gruffly.

As she took a closer look at the animal, she realized that

she'd never seen a cat like this one before. He looked feral and was close to two feet long with a very short tail.

"That's a bobcat."

"A young one?" she whispered.

"More like a teen. They don't get much bigger, but don't let their size fool you. Though not exactly in league with a mountain lion, they can do some serious damage to a human, particularly if you corner them."

He stepped in front of her. Then, standing rock still, he spoke softly in Navajo. The sound echoed eerily in the confines of the cave.

As she watched, the cat turned and walked away slowly and deliberately.

"It knows the way out," Luca said.

"Did you ask it to lead us out of here?" Nothing that Luca could do would surprise her anymore.

He shook his head. "I don't have that ability, though others do. What I did was thank Talking God and Black God, who taught the *Diné* how to hunt, for the animal they brought us. I asked that it be rewarded with long life for showing us the way out."

Luca followed the bobcat around a turn in the cavern. "If it'll make it easier for you, think of it this way. The cat doesn't have cubs to protect right now and doesn't want to fight us. He's being true to his nature by escaping. In the process, he'll lead us out of here, too."

All perfectly logical, yet Luca had managed to get the exact response he'd needed from the wild creature. She tried not to let her imagination run rampant, but the facts were hard to ignore. She'd never met anyone even remotely like Luca. Everything about him was extraordinary.

"There," he said, interrupting her thoughts. The bobcat had leaped up onto a ledge about four feet high. Above that was an opening in the hillside big enough to squeeze through.

Moments later they were out of the cave, trying to dry off in the sun. She brushed off her clothes, hoping she hadn't picked up any spiders along the way. She could face a grown man intent on killing her and never pause to do what was necessary, but spiders—the large, fuzzy ones—gave her the serious creeps.

She glanced at Luca, then back at the cemetery, which lay fifty feet below them toward the west. "We still haven't done what we came here to do," she said. "We need to go down and check those graves. Then we can get back to the car and turn on the heater."

"You're right. Let's finish the job."

More alert now since they knew about sinkholes, they checked the ground carefully before taking each step. Ten minutes later, they'd still found nothing of interest.

Disappointed, they were heading back downhill to the car when her cell phone rang. It was from the crime scene unit's team leader. "There's something you need to see for yourself," he said. "How soon can you get to the station?"

"We're on our way now. ETA thirty minutes," she answered.

Luca glanced at her as she put the phone away. "Did they turn up something on the car?"

"I think so, but we'll see," she said, repeating what she'd been told. "Our suspect's a crazy who's full of surprises, so we'll have to start looking around every corner. It's hard to fight what you can't see coming."

"I know this evil. I can equalize the odds against us."

As their gazes locked, Valerie felt the power behind the dark eyes that held hers. The same instinctive knowledge that told her he'd be a formidable adversary also assured her that he'd be an unforgettable lover. The tenderness of his kiss, and the magic it had woven around her, still burned in her mind.

"Thunderclouds are building quickly," Luca said, looking off into the distance.

She nodded, acknowledging what he'd said, but it was the storm raging inside of her that frightened her most.

"The wind's coming up, too. We won't be able to outrun this storm."

His words stayed in her mind. Run...that's what she'd always done when anyone got too close. But what she'd spent her life avoiding had now caught up to her.

Chapter Thirteen

It was after dark, but law enforcement work didn't keep regular hours and the evening shift was already busy. The uneasy silence that greeted them as they walked inside the department's automotive shop told her that Luca and she were in for some very disturbing news.

The senior mechanic, standing in an interior office with a window overlooking the service bays, saw them almost as they stepped into the garage and came out to join them. "I'm Bubba Dunlap," he said, introducing himself. "Whoever tampered with your car knew exactly what he was doing." He brought out photos of what they'd found beneath the car. "Two connections were loosened, not enough to trigger the sensors, but almost to the point of failure. The drive downhill and the extra stress on the hydraulic systems did the rest. It was deliberate—and skillful—sabotage."

There was more to the story, too. Luca could feel it in his gut. The way everyone kept glancing in their direction only served to confirm his suspicions.

"But there's something else the lead investigator insisted you see for yourself, providing you know about cars," he added.

"I do," Luca said. "I've worked on them from time to time."

Bubba rolled out a creeper and waved his hand. "Check out the spot on the frame just inboard from the jack point. You can't see it unless you get underneath."

Luca lay down on the creeper and rolled beneath the car. "I see a small square area, about the size of a pack of cigarettes, where there's no mud or dirt. Something was stuck there, but it must have dropped off after we left the road. Or it was removed."

"What was it?" she asked, looking over at Bubba.

"According to the tech who spotted the clear area, it was about the size of a GPS. The ground was searched, but it didn't come loose on its own. The tech thinks it was stuck on with a magnet because there's no glue or residue. My guess is that it was removed at the same time the brakes were tampered with. The team leader wanted you to see this for yourselves so that you'd remain on your guard."

"Thanks. At least we know that the new car's clean. We just got it," she answered, her voice taut.

Luca could feel her anger. She was practically vibrating with rage. The knowledge that someone had tampered with her car—and before that had been tracking them electronically—seriously pissed her off.

"We should go over the new car again. We spent some time away from it," Luca said.

"If we find anything, then he must have followed us after we switched cars and is probably disappointed that we didn't end up at the bottom of some ravine," she said with an edge in her voice as they walked toward the exit.

"Don't make it personal," he cautioned. "You'll lose perspective."

As they went outside to the parking lot, she brought a penlight out of her jacket pocket. "I just don't like being played for a fool."

"No one does." He, too, would have preferred to fight his enemy in the open—take a few blows while giving better than he got. But the one after them relished the shadows, and was growing stronger because of them.

As they reached the car, Luca moved ahead of her. "Let me take a look underneath."

"Good idea. If I found a GPS I'd be too tempted to smash it—in lieu of someone's face. Here, use my light."

Finding the jack point, he crawled under the driver's side. It only took him a moment and when he came back out, he was holding a small device in his hand. "It was in the same general area as before—held on by a magnet. We'll need to have this car checked for anything and everything—including the brake system. He had all the time in the world while we were down in that cave."

"We should've spotted the tail," she said, her lips stretched thin in anger.

"We were in a forest with a lot of blind spots, and with only few roads he didn't have to follow very close. He knew which direction we had to go, at least in general," he said. After a heartbeat he added, "But now it's our turn."

"What do you have in mind?" she asked.

"We become the hunters—instead of the hunted."

TAKING THE CAR into the garage to have it carefully examined gave them the opportunity to regroup. The GPS, which hadn't been deactivated, was currently being dusted for prints by a tech who'd walked over from the lab. This way whoever was tracking them wouldn't see the signal coming from somewhere the car couldn't possibly go. They wanted the suspect off his guard when they made their move.

While they waited, Luca and Valerie went across the street to a café many downtown workers patronized. It would be a late dinner, but the circumstances had finally provided them with time for a meal. Taking a seat at one of the corners of the large room, they ordered coffee and a sandwich and paid the tab when they were served, a common practice for officers on call.

"What we know so far is that the person after us is undoubtedly nuts, but he's also very intelligent," she said, thinking out loud. "He's proficient in Navajo ways, but he's also up on modern technology and knows how to tamper with brakes. He may have even grown up working on cars."

"I suspect that he's also enjoying himself. By keeping us looking over our shoulders, he diverts us from paying closer attention to the case," Luca said.

"Maybe it's Stephen Browning," she said, taking a bite out of her green chile burger, scarcely aware of its spicy heat.

"No, I don't think he's our man," Luca said after a beat. "But I think he's an important part of the puzzle. Maybe Browning's Navajo source is using him to keep tabs on what we're doing."

"What really worries me about our suspect is how easily he blends technology and cultural beliefs—and uses both to terrorize," Valerie said. "This is one scary dude."

"In this case, fear's a good thing. It'll make you more cautious."

"Do *you* fear him?" she asked, and saw his eyes flash with an emotion she couldn't easily define.

"What I feel isn't fear," he said slowly. "It's outrage. I want to collar this person who profanes our ways and desecrates everything I value. It's not just about justice—it's about restoring the *hózhq*."

Before she could reply, the tech who'd worked on their car entered the restaurant. He looked around, saw them, then walked over.

"The car's clean," he said, handing Valerie the keys. "The lab scanned from bumper to bumper for GPS signals and only got the one from the standard department unit. You might want to bring your vehicle in once a day for a quick scan, just to make sure it stays that way."

"That's not a bad idea," she said.

"That extra GPS is in the glove compartment—and it's still broadcasting the vehicle location. I was told you had plans to retain custody of it for a while."

"We do," Luca answered.

After the tech left, Valerie focused her attention back on Luca. "So now we lure this killer out into the open, someplace where we can take him down."

"Exactly."

Although that one word was spoken without inflection, she saw something deadly flicker in his eyes.

"I'm tired of playing by *his* rules," he added.

There was a change in him—a renewed determination to catch this suspect. Maybe it was pride—he hadn't liked becoming the killer's prey.

"He's upped his game. By sabotaging the brakes, he wasn't just playing with my life—he endangered you," Luca said, his voice as brittle and cold as ice.

The realization that it wasn't pride—it was protectiveness—hit her hard. A gentle warmth spiraled through her. Instantly aware of the turn her thoughts had taken, Valerie looked away and, searching for a distraction, took a final sip of coffee.

"This is our fight, and we won't lose," she said.

"No, we won't—and when it's over, you and I will celebrate…in ways we shouldn't think about now."

His voice was rough and his eyes held a dark edge. She stopped breathing and her heart leaped to her throat.

Fate was playing a joke on her. If she lowered her guard, Luca would steal her heart, then one day disappear from her life forever. Like it had been for her mother, she'd spend a lifetime sighing over what might have been.

"Let's go talk to the captain," Valerie said in a hardened voice as they left the café. "It's time to bait the trap."

Chapter Fourteen

Since the plan required close coordination and visual contact, they were forced to wait until the next afternoon. Their morning was spent catching up on paperwork and in meetings, ironing out the details of what would be a multijurisdictional operation.

When they finally set out at two-thirty, the GPS that had been planted on Valerie's unit was now in one of the cup holders. Unfortunately, the serial number had been scraped away and no fingerprints had been found on it. It all went to prove that their prey—seriously disturbed or not—was still able to think clearly enough not to leave evidence behind.

Valerie drove north on the interstate out of Albuquerque. An unmarked patrol unit with two plainclothes officers was behind them but staying well back. Two other patrol cars would follow on a parallel route. Their own departmental GPS system would allow them to know where every other unit was, keeping the operation from getting bunched up or spread too thin.

Ten minutes later, they turned west off the interstate, taking the exit to the east, then crossing over the highway west into the small city of Bernalillo. Soon they were heading south on a two-lane road.

Luca watched in the side mirror. "A white Ford sedan took the same exit off the interstate. Now it's looped around and coming our direction."

"Good eye. I'll call our backup and see if they can read the license plate." Valerie made a quick call on the tactical channel. "It appears that the same vehicle has been behind us all the way from Albuquerque, closing in then fading back. They're trying to get close enough now to read the plate."

"Let's hope we don't spook this guy…."

"Or lose our target, in case this vehicle isn't the right one," she added, completing his thought.

"He just took a right," Luca said, turning his head to look back. "It doesn't look like he was our tail after all."

"The vehicle's stolen," the dispatcher said, his voice coming over the radio clearly. "The tags don't match the description."

Valerie cursed under her breath. "He's either onto us, or we've stumbled across a car thief." She glanced into the rearview mirror, braked hard then slid the unit around in a moonshiner's turn. "Hang on!"

"He's back on the main highway, heading north again," Luca said. "We need to set up a roadblock before he gets to the freeway."

"I'll stay with the target. Call it in to the Sandoval County team. They're on standby and this is out of my jurisdiction," she said.

As Luca picked up the radio, he realized it was already too late to block the interstate. The white car screeched to the right again, racing south.

Luca called dispatch and instructed their parallel backup to block the frontage road ahead.

"They've got a spike belt, and time to place it," he said.

The white car had a good lead but Valerie, going over ninety already, was closing the gap.

Their prey slowed suddenly, brake lights flashing, then turned off the highway, pulling up beside an old pickup.

"He's making a run for it," Luca said, throwing the car door open and jumping out before they slid to a stop.

Ahead, a long-haired man wearing sunglasses, a stocking cap, baggy jeans and a loose-fitting shirt was sprinting down the wide ditch bank. He was racing directly toward an old man and a boy who were fishing in the clear irrigation ditch.

The fishermen turned in surprise just as the running suspect brushed by them hard, shoving them both into the water.

Luca was less than twenty-five yards from him when the suspect suddenly stopped, pulled out a gun and fired at him. Luca dodged to the left, barely missing a passing car.

Luca drew his own pistol, but as he glanced quickly to his right, he saw the boy in the ditch wildly waving his arms and fighting to stay above the waterline. The old man was in trouble, too.

The suspect fired again, the bullet whining past Luca. The shooter, now in the road, pointed his weapon at an approaching driver, obviously planning to hijack the man's vehicle.

Forced to decide between continuing pursuit or saving two innocent bystanders, Luca jammed his pistol back into his holster, dropped his borrowed cell phone on the ground then jumped into the twenty-foot-wide ditch feet-first. The boy's head was barely visible now. Luca made his way through the stream and had just grabbed hold of the Pueblo boy when Valerie ran up.

"Go after the suspect. I've got things here," he called out.

As she raced off, he pushed the boy out onto the steep bank. He then swam after the older man, who was clinging to a branch and trying to pull himself out of the water.

Moments later, father and son were on dry land. The shivering Pueblo man hugged his son tightly and tried to thank Luca.

"What you've done…" he said, his voice choked with emotion.

"My job, that's all," Luca said. Then, knowing they were okay, he took off, hoping to catch up to Valerie and the suspect.

Luca raced around a curve, still on the ditch bank. A hundred yards ahead Valerie was walking in his direction, talking on her cell phone. A man in a gray suit was following several feet behind her. He was also using a cell phone.

Seeing Luca, Valerie shook her head. "The perp carjacked

a blue sedan and kept going. I've called it in. The driver is Hubert Schultz, a salesman," she said, gesturing to the man behind her. "At least he wasn't hurt."

Schultz had stopped and was waving one of his arms in the air as he argued with someone.

"What did the victim see?" Luca asked, walking with Valerie back to the location where the civilians had been shoved into the irrigation canal.

"Mostly the muzzle of a gun. Mr. Schultz was told not to look at our suspect's face, so he complied. All I got from him was that the man's skin was dark, like an Indian or Hispanic. He was clean-shaven, his hair looked phony, like a wig, and his sunglasses looked expensive, not the drug-store kind. According to Schultz, the man was in his thirties, at least, and the stocking cap had a Lobo logo on it—UNM," she added.

"There must be thousands of those around. Mall Mart carries them even up in Farmington," Luca said. "But we still have the GPS, so the suspect's bound to surface again. He doesn't know we've found his tracking device. Of course all bets are off if he left the receiver in the car he abandoned back up the road."

"According to my last contact with dispatch, the Sandoval County deputies were going to check it out," she said, looking down the road. Two hundred yards away, a squad car was parked beside the abandoned white sedan, and officers were conducting a search.

A moment later, Valerie learned that their subject hadn't left anything important behind, like a GPS receiver.

"He must have taken the GPS with him. But we know what car he's driving at this moment and its license number," Luca pointed out.

"Right. Let me check and see if anyone's spotted Mr. Schultz's vehicle. I already gave dispatch the tag number," she said, punching a number on her cell phone.

The Tewa Pueblo man and his son came up to them just as

she ended the call. "My name is Lawrence Gonzales," he said. "I guess you were after that man for more than speeding?"

Luca nodded.

"Maybe I can help you then. Do you think that was the killer who profanes everything he touches?"

Luca nodded somberly, curious as to why the man had made that connection. He was about to ask when the man continued.

"I'm Tewa and so's my son. Like you, I'm *Ke,*" he said, still looking at Luca.

"I'm sorry, but I don't speak the language of your tribe," Luca said.

"I'm a medicine man," he answered. "*Ke* means Bear, and we're called that because at the time of the beginning, a bear was seen to treat its own wounds, like humans do."

"But I'm not a medicine man," Luca said, noting that the Tewa man was looking at the medicine bundle he carried on his belt.

Lawrence looked at Luca, surprised. "Strange. I felt… something…when you passed. A power."

"I'm a Navajo police detective on special assignment." As he spoke, Luca realized that the fetish in his pocket felt heavier than usual. Aware that it would need tending to since he'd gone into the water, Luca brought the cougar out of the *jish* and dried it off.

This time, instead of placing it back in its pouch, he removed one of the leather strands that held the pouch closed, looped it around the fetish and hung the cougar around his neck.

As Luca glanced at the Tewa medicine man he saw him smile. "You're a hunt chief, or as we call them, *Pi xen,*" Lawrence said, "but you're even more than that…. You're what we know as *tsiwi,* those with the sweeping eyes, a predator against witches. Your spiritual brother, the cougar, will hunt with you as you continue your search for the witch—and you *will* win."

"I won't give up until I do," Luca said with a nod.

"You helped my son and me. Now let me repay you."

"It's not needed—" Luca began, but the Tewa man held up one hand.

"The *Diné* believe in balance and harmony. Let me honor that."

They followed him to his pickup, which had been parked across the road and gone unnoticed until now. There, Lawrence Gonzales reached for a small wooden box he kept behind the driver's seat.

"This will help you complete your task," he said, taking out two feathers. "They're from a red-tailed hawk and will allow you to move with the silence and speed of that bird of prey, and spot a witch even in total darkness. Your *Po wa ha*, the spirit of the fetish you carry, will help you do the rest."

"Sir, you came closer to the suspect than either of us," Valerie said. "We know about the hair color, stocking cap and sunglasses. Is there anything else you can add to that description now that things have calmed down?"

He nodded then spoke. "He had a dried blue lizard hanging from a string around his neck. The gallbladder of a blue lizard is used for poisoning people, and that's how I knew who— and what—he was. After that, I was in the water and didn't see anything else."

"And you?" She glanced down at the seven-year-old by his side.

"He had long hair. I tried to grab it when he pushed my dad, and it moved. So I think it was a wig," the boy replied. "Then he pushed *me* into the ditch." The boy's eyes grew large, the memory of fear imprinted there clearly. "I don't know how to swim," he added, in a whisper-thin voice.

Luca smiled at him. "You did real good in there keeping your head above water."

It wasn't uncommon for kids in the desert not to know how to swim, and Luca had a feeling the skinwalker had known that, too. The witch had deliberately knocked the boy and his dad into the water, betting that Luca would do the right thing and try to save the innocents.

This skirmish was over, but they'd have another chance to do battle soon enough. Luca could feel that certainty inside him as clearly as the sun's warmth.

As Luca glanced at Valerie, another gentler emotion coursed through his veins. Her softness, her courage and even her determination not to give up sang to him without words. It called to him, urging him to protect this woman from an evil that went beyond anything she'd ever known, or even imagined.

Chapter Fifteen

As they walked back to the car, Valerie thought about what had just happened with the Tewa man and his son. Luca's courage knew few limits, and he commanded respect from everyone he met. It was little wonder that she was so drawn to him.

Although she hadn't wanted to work with a partner, she was now glad that Luca had been assigned to the case. She'd never admit it aloud, but this wasn't her kind of fight. The witchcraft stuff…it just made her uneasy.

As they got into the car, her cell phone rang. "We've located the blue sedan," Captain Harris said. "The suspect abandoned it by the railroad tracks on the northern outskirts of Albuquerque, in county, where we had that string of burglaries last year."

"Any sign of him in the area?" Valerie asked.

"We haven't received any calls about another carjacking, so we think he's still on foot in the neighborhood. But that area's not a great place for the uninvited."

He didn't have to elaborate. The neighborhood was known for its vigilante group, one that patrolled its streets and took the law into its own hands more often than not. Although euphemistically called the neighborhood association, they were big trouble to anyone who dared create problems for the area residents.

A kid who'd been breaking into trucks and selling whatever

he could steal had eluded the sheriff department's best efforts to catch him. Fed up, the association had gone to work. A few days later, deputies had found the suspect naked, bound and gagged in an abandoned warehouse filled with hot merchandise of all types. Fingerprints had sealed the case against the boy.

"We're heading there next," Valerie told Captain Harris.

"You've still got the GPS with you?" he asked.

"Yeah, I'm keeping it with the unit. Let this wacko tail us again. There's nothing my partner and I would like better than another shot at the prize," Valerie said.

"If he hasn't ditched the GPS tracker, he'll be able to spot you coming—and know exactly where you are," Captain Harris warned.

"We'll leave the GPS in my vehicle and work on foot," she said.

Valerie ended the call, then closed the phone with one hand and filled Luca in. "The area we're heading into plays by its own rules. Their calls to the department often require a forty-five-minute response time, so residents learned to take care of things without outside help."

"Reading between the lines, what you're really saying is that if they spot a stranger they think will create trouble, like maybe our suspect, they'll lean pretty hard on him?" he asked with a grim smile.

"Yeah, like that. They're just not too friendly. The last time I had to go in there I couldn't get any cooperation whatsoever. All I got was a lot of stares and the strong feeling that they wanted me out of their neighborhood."

It was late afternoon by the time she parked in front of a small pueblo-style house. The yard contained several large tables filled with junk, like an abandoned yard sale. "We need to work quickly to see if anyone has noticed our suspect. Once it gets dark, it'll be easier for him to slip away."

"Do you think he'd just call a cab?" Luca asked.

"I thought of that, and I have a deputy checking with the cab companies. But I don't think he'd want a cabbie to be able to ID him to officers. My guess is that he'll hide out in somebody's storage shed until dark then try and pick his way out of the area on foot."

He nodded. "Makes sense. Why don't you work the east side of the street, and I'll work the west? At the end of each block, we'll touch base and share what we've learned."

"Sounds like a plan." She placed the GPS in the glove compartment after he exited, then they got to work.

Luca couldn't get anyone to answer the door at the first house, so he looked around the side and listened to see if there was anyone around. A dog barked behind the wooden fence and through the slits he saw fangs.

As he went to the front again, he saw a child peek out from behind a curtain then get pulled back out of view. It had only taken seconds, but in that time Luca had caught a glimpse of Navajo talking prayersticks. The bundle, wrapped with colorful yarn, had caught his attention immediately. Those particular prayersticks were carried for personal protection by Navajos away from the Rez.

Walking back to the front door, Luca identified himself in Navajo and held out his badge near the peephole. Several minutes later a young Navajo woman wearing jeans and a sweatshirt opened the door. Luca addressed her in Navajo and soon learned she hadn't heard or seen anyone. Taking care of an active two-year-old took all her focus and attention. Luca continued down the sidewalk and strode up to the next house.

TWO HOURS LATER, it was getting close to dark and they'd still failed to get a lead of any kind. Most of the people, including the few Navajos he'd met, had been very guarded around him, and more concerned about his presence in their neighborhood. One middle-aged Hispanic man had even questioned his badge, convinced it was a fake, and had ordered him to move on.

They continued canvassing the area, and eventually entered an old trailer court with four rows of mobile homes, many of them in need of major repairs. Judging by their age and condition, people here were just getting by.

The first two homes were deserted as a quick look inside their small, curtainless windows confirmed. Moving on, Luca noted a Navajo Tribal Rodeo bumper sticker on the ten-year-old pickup parked beside the third house. As he drew near the front door, the scent of fresh fry bread filled the air and made his mouth water.

Luca knocked and identified himself, but nobody responded. Going around the back to a half-glass patio door, he knocked then cupped his hands on both sides of his head and peered inside.

"Whatcha doing peeping in windows, pervert?" a husky Navajo in jeans and a T-shirt growled, coming around the corner of the home. He had a big rake in his hands, raised and ready to strike.

"*Yáat'ééh,* friend," Luca said. "Put down the rake, please. I'm a Navajo police officer."

"Long way from the Rez, aren't you? Or do you have a problem with geography?" he countered. "I'm the captain of this neighborhood association, and if you move an inch, I'll bounce you off the wall."

Two more Navajo men appeared from around the same corner. One had a big folding knife, and the other was carrying a roofing hammer, the double-headed kind with a hatchet side. "Way to go, Hoskie. You caught the pervert."

"Hold on. Let me show you my badge," Luca said, reaching slowly toward his pocket.

"He's got a gun!" the man with the rake shouted, swinging it at Luca's head.

Luca slipped to the side, throwing up his arm. The tool bounced off with only a glancing blow and struck the metal sidewall of the trailer. The handle splintered with a loud crack.

Luca knew he couldn't draw his weapon here. Even a hit could pass through an attacker and kill an innocent bystander in one of the mobile homes. Grabbing the half of the rake handle still in the man's hands, he kicked his attacker in the chest and knocked him back. Although the handle was longer than the nightstick he'd been trained to use back at the academy, it would serve to fend off his attackers.

The slender man with the knife took a swipe with his blade next, but Luca was able to block the move with the oak handle and almost succeeded in knocking the knife from the man's hand.

"Be careful," a woman yelled from inside the house. "He could be the evil one the police have been searching for. Don't let him witch you."

"I'm *not* the evil one," Luca yelled out, slamming the man waving the hatchet across the wrist. "But that man *did* come this way about an hour ago. We tracked the car he stole to this location. I'm here to hunt him down," Luca explained in a rush, keeping the staff moving to ward off the two weapons still threatening him. "I've got medicine to protect me."

"Liar! You're him!" The big man reached for the rake handle, but Luca jabbed him in the chest with the blunt end, sending him stumbling back with a gasp.

Out of the corner of his eye Luca detected movement from beside the house just as the man with the hatchet cocked it back to throw.

With a yell, Valerie suddenly leaped the remaining six feet and tackled the man to the ground. Rolling away quickly, she scrambled to her feet. When the man grabbed her shoulders, she kicked him in the groin. He gasped, then doubled up and fell to the ground.

One of the other men grabbed her arm and swung her around, bouncing her off the wall. Valerie recaptured her balance quickly and pressed her back to the trailer. As two more neighborhood men moved in, she knew that she was in for the fight of her life.

Suddenly Luca was there beside her. She'd never seen a man move so fast or fight so effectively in her life. Two more men went down, but the entire neighborhood was now turning out, eager to join the fight.

Suddenly there was a loud, ear-shattering whistle. Everyone stopped dead in their tracks and turned around to look.

A tall Navajo man in his late sixties stood at the street curb. "Stop," he ordered in a calm, resolute tone.

While she and Luca held their ground, the men they'd been fighting stepped back, allowing the newcomer to approach.

Catching her breath, Valerie spoke quickly. "My name's Detective Jonas, and I'm with the Bernalillo County Sheriff's Department. If you'll let me reach for my badge, I can prove it."

"Keep your hand away from that holster," a man holding a crowbar growled.

"It's all right. Let her show her identification," the older Navajo man said.

There was something about him that compelled the others to obey. The man had presence, she'd give him that. He'd meet any challenge to his authority with a cold glare that made any hint of opposition fade instantly.

The man looked down at Luca's medicine bundle, then studied his face for a moment. *"Hasih."*

"Bideelni," Luca answered, relief on his face.

She wasn't sure what had just happened, but the tension that had surrounded them dissipated instantly. The old man nodded to the others and immediately the men retreated. Moments later only he, Luca and Valerie remained.

"We should go back to my home," the man said. "Even our streets aren't safe enough after dark."

"Uncle, we would appreciate your hospitality. My partner's bleeding," Luca said.

Valerie glanced down at herself and wasn't surprised to see her shirt streaked and dotted with blood splatters. Her hands and left arm had some minor cuts and scrapes, and when she touched a tender spot on her cheek her finger came back moist. Although her entire body ached, she found some satisfaction in the fact that most of the blood on her clothing had come from her assailants.

"I'll live," she said with a quick half smile.

"Yes, you will," the man answered, smiling back at her. "I'm known as *Deez*." He lifted his arm and showed them the scars left by a bad burn. "It means singed."

She nodded but didn't comment. Hoping either *Deez* or Luca would explain the connection between them, she waited. They'd obviously recognized each other. But when *Deez* didn't volunteer any further information and Luca remained silent, she curbed her curiosity, opting to wait for now.

Several minutes later they arrived at a small pueblo-style stucco home in a cul-de-sac. A smaller structure that resembled the first stood at the back of the property. Casitas. They were often used as guest homes or in-law quarters. Sometimes, they became home offices or workshops.

There was a bright porch light on at the main house, and Valerie could see the place was well tended, with bright yellow sunflowers framing the entryway.

They were inside the main house a moment later. Valerie and Luca remained standing, reluctant to sit because of the dirt and debris on their clothing. *Deez* insisted, however, then offered them some cold herbal tea. Though Valerie normally wouldn't have accepted anything like that from someone she didn't know, particularly someone connected to a case, there was something about *Deez* that assured her he could be trusted. Luca, too, seemed very relaxed around him.

"It's getting late now, and you've been through a lot tonight. You shouldn't drive again until you've had time to rest. My wife and I use the casita out back for friends and relatives who drop by. You can rest there till morning if you wish."

"There's no need—" she started, but then saw Luca shake his head.

"We will accept, Uncle," he said. "There's no place safer than where we are."

Considering that they'd nearly been beaten within an inch of their lives, Valerie could have argued the point—but didn't.

As *Deez* went to get some keys, Luca explained. "He's from a well-respected tribal organization," he said, deliberately not mentioning the Brotherhood by name. "To turn down his hospitality would be an insult." Seeing she still wasn't convinced, he added, "And it might cost us crucial information."

Considering she was exhausted and ached everywhere, Valerie nodded, deciding to go along with it for now.

A short time later *Deez* escorted them to the casita. It was meticulously clean, and fresh flowers were on a vase on the dining-area table. Everything appeared to have been readied for guests.

"You were expecting company tonight?" Valerie asked, wondering if they were upsetting his plans.

"No, but since unplanned guests often drop by, my wife and I keep things ready here just in case," he answered. "Go ahead and make yourself comfortable. In the meantime, Nephew, you and I should talk."

As Valerie glanced around she noticed the bathtub just beyond the open bathroom door. A long soak…that's just what she needed.

"We have clothing inside the closet," *Deez* said. "Help yourself to anything that fits you."

"Oh, I wouldn't—"

He smiled and shook his head. "That's why they're there—for unexpected company."

Although she wondered about that, every muscle in her body ached badly and she was too tired to care. A long soak… Afterward she'd ask.

Deez said something to Luca in Navajo. Then after making sure she'd have everything she might need, he and Luca went back to the main house.

Alone at last, Valerie checked in with her captain via cell phone, giving him a brief report and catching up on news from the crime scene—which, so far, was unchanged.

After ending the call, Valerie slipped out of her clothes while the bathtub filled up with hot water, then eased in. The warmth soothed her aching muscles. There was no better prescription for what ailed her.

Resting her head against the edge of the tub, she closed her eyes and allowed her thoughts to drift. Too many things were happening in her life and it was all coming at her at the speed of light. She'd always run as fast as she could from love. She, of all people, knew that emotion for the cheat it was. Love weakened you in a world where only the strong survived. Yet around Luca, love became a constant temptation that demanded her surrender.

Her eyes popped open. Whoa…who said anything about love? Taking a deep breath, she closed them again. She was just tired. A long soak would eventually unscramble her brains.

LUCA MET WITH *Deez* in the main house. He was more curious than ever about the man. He hadn't expected to meet a member of the Brotherhood here and now.

"I see the questions in your eyes," *Deez* said, waving him to a chair. "But meeting a brother shouldn't have surprised you. All of us here in the metro area were put on alert, given the code words and told to help you if the situation arose."

"Without you today…" Luca shook his head. He didn't have to continue. *Deez* knew.

"Nephew, people are very scared. Even *Diné* who would normally respect another member of the tribe might turn on you now if they don't know you. People go on the offensive when they're afraid."

"I saw," he said, nodding.

"I've been told to let you know that you'll have backup close by—within fifteen to twenty minutes—no matter where you are in the county. But trust *no one* outside our circle—and never lower your guard." He paused for several long moments and silence stretched out between them. At long last, he spoke again. "The woman with you…I sense you have feelings for her."

He started to deny it, then stopped. "She's my partner in this investigation."

"There's more to it than that, though you may not be ready to define it yet," *Deez* said slowly. "But remember that even though she has proven to be a good ally, she doesn't really understand what you're fighting."

Luca thought of the way she'd jumped in, stood her ground and fought beside him. She'd risked her life to save his. It was what partners did for each other. Yet, in this case, it was that—and more.

"The detective should have called for backup first but instead she rushed forward to help you," *Deez* added, voicing Luca's unspoken thoughts. "She led with her heart instead of her head, a dangerous tactic."

"It happened so fast she had no time to think things through. She reacted instinctively," he argued, though in his own heart he knew *Deez* was right.

Deez said nothing for a moment. "Watch yourself. Emotions can complicate your assignment and lead to mistakes when you can least afford them."

"Understood." Luca absently rubbed the back of his neck, then his bruised bicep, where he'd taken a glancing blow from the rake handle.

"But now you're tired, and it's understandable after what you've been through. Go rest. You're safe here."

Luca thanked him then headed back to the casita, tired and needing a rest. As he walked in through the front door, he called Valerie's name, mostly to let her know who it was. But only silence greeted him.

Anticipating trouble, his body immediately tensed and he drew his weapon. A search of the casita revealed that she wasn't in the house. As his glance took in the bedroom dresser, he saw her badge and gun.

Fear shot through him, though there were no signs of a struggle in any of the rooms. Moving silently and cautiously, he stepped into the shadows.

Spotting a flicker of movement in the darkness up ahead, he moved toward it, then heard the rustle of leaves and a gasp of pain.

He wasn't sure how he knew, but he was certain it had come from Valerie. Luca crept forward, ready to fight, but as he rounded the corner someone kicked him in the back of the knees. He went down hard.

Chapter Sixteen

Luca rolled and tackled his opponent to the ground. In an instant, he moved on top of him, fist back, ready to punch.

"*What* are you doing creeping around out here?" an all-too-familiar voice demanded. "It's me. Now get off."

A wave of relief washed over him as he recognized Valerie's voice. "I thought you were in trouble," he said, but didn't move away. He liked the feel of her below him and wanted to enjoy it for a few seconds more. "What are *you* doing out here?"

"I was going to sit down and enjoy the cool night air. I tried to drag the chair over here, but my muscles weren't up to it. Then you sneaked up on me—but I didn't know it was you," she said, her heart pounding and her voice breathy.

She wanted him. Everything male in him knew it. Valerie shifted below him, and as he slid into the cradle of her thighs, needs exploded inside him.

Luca gazed down at her and saw her lips part. That invitation pushed him over the edge. He brought his mouth down roughly over hers, greedily taking everything.

With a soft moan, she surrendered, melting into his kiss. "More," she managed.

The pressure tightening the lower part of his body was making him crazy, and her plea only fueled the heat pulsing through him. "In another second there won't be any turning back," he warned, his breath hot over her moistened lips.

"That second's passed," she whispered, her words nothing more than a sigh. "It's too late for you—and for me."

Desire and passion shimmered in the warmth of her eyes. Wrapping his arms around her, he rose to his feet and carried her back inside.

As he held her against him, she slipped her hand inside the folds of his shirt. A shudder tore through him as he felt her soft caress.

"Don't do that. Not yet. Patience," he said, sucking in a breath.

He wanted to take her hard and fast, forgetting everything but the fire burning inside him. But he had to hold back. She needed…more.

Setting her down before him, he kissed her slowly, then with practiced hands worked her shirt open. The realization that she was wearing no underwear shot through him like a high-voltage current.

He pulled the fabric down her shoulders, trapping her arms and pinning her against him. Raw needs blasting through him, he found her breast, nipped at the soft tip then soothed it with his tongue.

Valerie cried out his name, melting against him and begging for more. "I want you," she managed, clinging desperately to him.

"Not yet, we're just beginning." In one deft movement, he undid her jeans and slipped them downward, his hands tracing the soft outline of her hips. "Lean on my shoulders," he ordered, and knelt before her parted legs. Opening her to him, he tasted her sweetness.

The way she responded nearly broke him. Her muffled cries rang in his ears. When he felt her grow too weak to stand, he lifted her into his arms and set her down on the bed.

He tore off his clothes, crazy with needs. But before he could lay over her, Valerie shifted and moved on top of him.

"I want to memorize everything about you," she murmured, loving the way he shuddered when she ran her hands over him.

"Stop," he growled. "You don't realize what you're doing to me."

"I *want* you to lose control," she whispered, driving him wild with gentle, warm kisses that burned through his skin and melted into his soul. She touched him everywhere, then at long last her hand closed in over him. His eyes darkened impossibly and he sucked in a ragged breath.

With a groan that came from deep inside him, he grasped both her hands, pinned her back onto the mattress, and pushed himself into her. Mindless now, he knew nothing but the sensations that were driving him to lose himself in her.

Valerie responded to his every thrust, opening herself even more to him.

Engulfed in waves of pleasure, their bodies rocked together, and with his heartbeat roaring in his head, he poured himself into her.

An eternity later, bathed in the wonderful afterglow, sanity slowly returned. "It'll never be the same between us," she murmured nuzzling into him.

"Regrets?" he managed, his voice steadier now.

"None," she answered. "Tonight, we belong to each other."

"And tomorrow…is a new day," he said at last, finishing her unspoken thought.

Nestled safely against him, she pushed away logic and the whispered warnings at the back of her mind. Until daybreak, she'd remain in this beautiful world they'd created together and enjoy the warmth.

THE NEXT MORNING while she still slept, Luca rose to greet the dawn. As his Song filled the air, he took a pinch of pollen from his *jish* and made the offering. "Now all is well," he chanted, finishing the prayer.

When he turned around, Valerie was standing there in the doorway, watching him. She was already dressed, and as he looked into her eyes, he saw an uncharacteristic trace of uncertainty in the gentle, soft woman he'd loved so intimately the night before.

Her phone rang. She spoke hurriedly. After she finished she turned her attention back to him. Instantly, he saw the change in her. His gut tightened. All he could see before him now was his partner, the police detective.

"We need to get going," she said, her tone crisp and businesslike. "Captain Harris said that the trace evidence recovered from both cars the perp drove was no help."

"What did they find?" he asked, his tone as impersonal and detached as hers.

"A few prints. They're being traced, but unless the suspect's in the system, that won't help us at all until we have him in custody. The white car the suspect used to follow us was stolen the day before from a mall parking lot. Deputies are checking surveillance video, hoping to get lucky, but the ball's back in our court now. And Harris made it clear he expects us to make progress soon."

From her attitude it was clear she was looking for a way to create distance between them. And she was right. They wouldn't be able to function effectively as police detectives without it.

His feelings for Valerie were strong, just one more reason for him to pull back. His work remained a big part of who he was, and there was no room for anything else in his life despite the cost. He'd failed one woman he'd loved. He wouldn't risk that again.

"I've already picked up our stuff and left some money to help pay for the clothing we took from *Deez's* closet. Should we leave a note?" Valerie asked.

"That's not necessary," *Deez* said.

She jumped, surprised, and turned around. "I never heard you come up."

"You were focused on something else," he answered with a smile. "Let's go inside the house. There are things you need to know before you leave."

COFFEE CUPS IN HAND, they sat around the wooden bench-style kitchen table. *Deez* had insisted on making them breakfast, and hungry, they'd accepted.

Valerie studied Luca and *Deez*. Though she couldn't put her finger on what it was, there was a connection between the two men that went beyond race.

Despite everything Luca and she had shared, he remained a man of secrets. Before she could give that much thought, Luca glanced at her.

"I think we should go talk to them," he said, interrupting her thoughts.

"Two of those Navajo students live in rentals just down the block," *Deez* added. "They catch the bus to the university from the next street over."

Wishing she'd paid more attention to the first part of their conversation, Valerie remained quiet and looked at one man then the other hoping someone would fill in the gaps.

"Some of our young people are fascinated by the old ways. They've asked me about the evil ones many times, too. They say they study all that at the college." *Deez* shook his head and grew silent for several long moments. "Maybe one of them has been enticed by the power the dark ones have," he added in a sad voice. "It happens, especially to the naive or disenchanted."

"Out of those students you spoke about, is there one who seems most likely to go down that path?" Valerie asked, instantly focused.

He shrugged. "You'll have to decide that for yourself. I've spoken to their college professor, Dr. Becenti, and warned him about openly discussing certain things, but he didn't listen to me. He kept insisting that his academic integrity demanded that he teach the course his own way."

"What was your overall impression of Dr. Becenti?" Valerie asked.

The old man hesitated. "He knows a lot about the Navajo

ways," *Deez* admitted slowly, "but it's knowledge from the head and not the heart."

"So overall, you'd rather see someone else teaching that class?" Valerie pressed.

"Yes. Teaching others the Navajo Way is much more than presenting facts for students to memorize. Professor Becenti hasn't been able to accept who he is—not fully Anglo and not fully Navajo—and that slants his perspective on what he's attempting to teach."

Valerie nodded, wondering if she'd ever find balance in her own life. She'd spent half of her life proving that she was as good as any man and hiding her feminine side, seeing it as a weakness others could exploit. Yet last night in Luca's arms she'd discovered the power of gentleness.

She shook free of the thought. *Not now.* "Let's go talk to the students."

Together with *Deez* they made their way down the block to a rundown version of *Deez's* home and waited by the low block wall that surrounded the property. Soon a young woman wearing the Traditional long skirt and a loose-fitting blouse came to the door. She waved, inviting them to approach.

"Uncle, it's good to see you," she said, looking at *Deez.* "I heard about the trouble last night and was hoping you hadn't been caught up in all that."

"I'm fine," *Deez* assured.

Stepping in front of Valerie, *Deez* went inside the house first, then Luca. Valerie followed last.

The young woman smiled at Valerie as they entered together. "Our men don't step aside and wait for women to lead. They always go first in case there's trouble," she added softly.

Valerie smiled, understanding now what had seemed odd to her before.

"My name's Ann Tapahonso," she said, looking at Valerie, then Luca. "I've got a lot to learn about the old ways, but I'm working hard to make up for lost time. I don't think I'll ever be a Traditionalist, but I hope, at least, to make a good New Traditionalist."

Deez glanced at Valerie and, with a grin, explained, "It's our own name for the *Diné* who follow as many of the old ways as is convenient. They have hogans and cable TV."

The young woman laughed. "Well, yeah. But I happen to like cable TV."

"We'd like to ask you a few questions," Luca said, taking the lead. "I understand that you're taking a university class on the old ways. Who's in the class and how many students are enrolled?"

"One dropped out after a few weeks, so there's about ten of us now. The majority are Navajos who grew up off the Rez and wanted to know more about our own culture." She paused, then continued. "Most of us have learned to adapt to the Anglo world, but we still battle prejudice daily, and it's easier to do that when you know who you are."

Deez nodded.

Ann paused another moment before continuing. "Dr. Becenti at the college really understands that, too. He's part Navajo but was raised like an Anglo and had to fight hard to claim a place for himself in both worlds."

"To your knowledge, does anyone in the group believe the Navajo Way has too many taboos and restrictions?" Luca asked.

"You're looking for the evil one," she said with a thoughtful nod. "But most of us respect the limits—" Ann stopped speaking abruptly and looked down at her shoes.

"But not *all* of you feel that way," Luca said, sensing what she'd left unsaid.

"Some of us want to be more than what we are," she said quietly. "Like *Cháala,*" she said, then looked at Valerie. "It means Charlie."

"Tell us about him," Valerie said.

"He lives just down the street. I've been told that he's tried several times to become a *hataalii,* but to do that you have to apprentice and memorize many Sings. He's not interested in all that, so he keeps trying to fast-track the whole thing." Glancing at the clock on the wall, she quickly added, "I'm sorry, but I have to go. I have a class in less than an hour."

After saying goodbye to her, *Deez,* Valerie and Luca met out on the sidewalk.

"Do you know who she was talking about, this wannabe *hataalii?*" Luca asked *Deez.*

He nodded. "*Cháala* Tso is a part-time student at the university, but I don't think he's your man."

"Why?" Valerie asked.

"He respects our teachings at least enough to avoid contamination with the dead. A few weeks ago Mrs. Salas and her husband were in a car accident. He died in her arms. Since then, *Cháala* goes around the block just to avoid her. He may not be a *hataalii,* but he doesn't disregard our ways or subvert them like an evil one would," he said. Noting the position of the sun, he added, "Nephew, I have to leave you now. I'm expected elsewhere this morning."

"Go, Uncle, and thank you very much for all the help you've given us," Luca said.

"There's one more thing," he said in a low, thoughtful voice. "I'm no crystal gazer, but I can sometimes foretell things that have yet to happen." *Deez* looked somberly at Luca then at Valerie. "You've both embarked on a difficult journey. Blood will be spilled and everything you've ever believed about yourselves, and each other, will be tested. In the end, neither of you will ever be the same," he said in a heavy voice, then walked away before either could ask him more.

Valerie glanced at Luca. "What do you think that means?"

Luca took a deep breath then let it out slowly. "You tell me."

Even without looking directly at her, he sensed that she'd understood *Deez,* just as he had. Though they were both determined to deny their feelings, it was too late to turn back the clock.

Blocking those thoughts for now, Luca glanced up the street. "I say we go pay *Cháala* a visit. He's at the third house down."

"Wait a minute. *How* could you possibly know that?"

"See that three-foot-high mound of rocks by the side of the front porch?" he answered.

She squinted and eventually nodded.

"It's for success on a journey. In this case, I imagine it's a journey of discovery. There's also that buckskin pollen bag hanging from a nail on the post framing the porch. That's to protect his home."

"Okay, let's go talk to him."

As they walked over, Valerie glanced at him. "There's a special connection between you and *Deez*. That's the main reason we stayed in one piece after we encountered those angry neighbors. Right?"

He said nothing, but this time she refused to accept his silence and pressed him. "Am I right?" she repeated.

"Yes."

"It's not just because you're both Navajo either."

This time he didn't answer. Some secrets were not his to share.

Chapter Seventeen

They were in front of the second house when Luca's pace slowed. Valerie noticed it instantly. "What's up?" she asked in a soft voice meant for his ears only.

"I caught a glimpse of someone following us. He's about twenty-five yards back, across the street and standing beside that white pickup."

"The GPS was never turned back on, right?" Valerie verified.

"Right." Luca reached up to touch the fetish around his neck. "I don't sense danger, but someone's back there, watching."

"Let's cross the street and go past the trash bin in front of the house that's being renovated. I'll duck down and hide behind it while you go around the side of the house. We'll trap him between us."

"Good plan. Let's go," he said.

A few tense minutes later, Steve Browning strode past her hiding place. Muttering a curse, Valerie burst out from her cover and confronted him. "Browning, I'm beginning to think you have a death wish. How did you find us?"

"I'd heard that you'd followed a suspect into this area last night. You also called the department this morning," he added with a shrug.

Valerie's eyes narrowed. "I reported it in, but it wasn't by radio. Who told you where we'd be?"

He smiled and shook his head. "You know better than to ask me that."

Someone at the station was leaking information to him, and although it ticked her off big-time, there was nothing she could do about it—at least for now.

"So what's up? Were you on your way to question *Cháala,* the future *hataalii?*" he asked.

"How did you know about him?" Valerie countered.

"You spoke to Ann earlier. She and I were…friends for a long time. These days we're both too busy with other things, but we stay in touch."

"What do you know about *Cháala?*" Valerie demanded as Luca came up from behind to join them.

"I've met him a few times, and spoke to him on the phone recently. His full name's Charlie Tso. He's heard about the skinwalker murders—that has a ring to it, don't you think?— and wants to protect the neighborhood. He's been going on foot patrols every night. He's sure that his own magic will protect him. And who knows? Maybe it would from a skin- walker, but it won't do much against a mugger. In his shoes, I'd also be carrying a gun."

"We're going over to talk to him now and I want you out of our way. Am I clear?"

"Sure. It's like I told you. All I want is the story."

Valerie and Luca headed to the house, and as they arrived, Luca stopped at the curb by the mailbox.

"If we want to get anything from him, we're going to have to wait out here until he invites us in," Luca said. "I'm assuming he's taken up at least some Traditionalist ways."

"Okay, we'll wait." Valerie stared down the street, lost in thought. "Do you think *Cháala* will turn out to be the perp?" She glanced back at the house before them, then shook her head. "Never mind. Things are *never* that simple."

Before Luca could comment, a stocky, young Navajo man opened the door. Standing in the entrance, he motioned for them to approach.

As they reached the porch, Luca saw the prayersticks in each of the two corners closest to the door.

"I knew you were here in our neighborhood," *Cháala* said, looking at Luca. "I've heard about you."

"About me, or about what happened last night?" Luca countered.

"Both. I know about last night. It's not surprising since everyone's on guard because of the evil one that's on the loose. But I also know about you and your brothers," he finished. "You, and they, helped a cousin of mine back on the Rez several months ago. He's a Modernist who goes by the same of Sam Pete. He'd been accused of working with a group of Anglos who were stealing cultural artifacts. You all helped him clear his name."

"I remember the case," Luca said, eager to finish this before *Cháala* revealed much more.

"Without the work all of you—"

"I understand," Luca said, interrupting him. As he glanced at Valerie, he knew it was already too late. Her curiosity and investigative mind were already working overtime. She knew that it wasn't like him to interrupt anyone, and the second he'd done that she had made a mental note of it. He cursed silently, wondering how to duck the questions she was sure to be asking him later. Curiosity wasn't enough to warrant revealing one of the tribe's most guarded secrets. The Brotherhood would have to remain the stuff of legend to her.

"The evil one you're after has some very real powers," *Cháala* continued. "That's how he's managed to elude the police, despite all their modern equipment and manpower."

"We're getting closer every hour," Valerie said. "We'll catch the creep."

Luca knew pride when he heard it, and so did Tso.

"The real problem is that the Sheriff's Department doesn't understand what it's fighting," Tso said.

"So why don't you enlighten us?" Valerie said.

"He hides under the skin of a coyote, the Trickster, and can run as fast as lightning."

"So you've seen him?" Valerie asked instantly.

Tso shook his head. "I don't know *who* he is, just *what* he is." He looked at Luca. "And so do you. That's why you're here."

Luca nodded once. "Do *you* have any idea who could be behind the deaths? Ritual killings like these require specialized knowledge."

The young man considered it for several moments. "*Deez* would know what's necessary, but that man respects our ways. I'm sure he's not responsible. I know something about those evil practices, too, but I'm not guilty either." He suddenly glanced at Luca. "Is that why you came here? You thought I might be the evil one?"

"I discarded you as a possible suspect once I saw the wards around your home. You wouldn't have had those in place if you were the one I was after," Luca said. "We're hoping you'll be able to tell us about the other anthropology students and suggest a possible suspect."

"I wish I could help, but the students in our class are just people searching for their cultural identity. They want to know who they are. The evil one…he already knows who and what he is."

"If you wanted to mimic the work of an evil one, where would you go to find the necessary details and information?" Valerie asked him, playing a hunch.

Cháala thought about it carefully before answering. "I'd ask the older ones back on the Rez. Come to think of it, they may not be willing to give away that knowledge. A better bet would be the professors at the college who specialize in that field. I'd check on the Internet, too, though I'm not sure how much accurate information is out there."

The young man paused, but they both could see that he was still thinking, so neither of them interrupted.

"There's an Anglo reporter who has been coming around after class. He teaches at the university, too. His name's Steve Browning. He's been asking everyone who even looks Navajo about the practices of an evil one. I was there when Browning asked Dr. Becenti about the blowpipes the evil ones are said to use," *Cháala* said, then looked at Luca and in a guarded whisper added, "Browning worries me. When *Deez* threw out his trash a few days ago, I saw him going through it. *Deez* had just cut his hair, too."

Valerie looked at Luca, puzzled, but didn't interrupt as *Cháala* continued.

Tso stood. "I better get going or I'll be late for work. I have a job at the university bookstore. It helps me cover my expenses."

As they left Tso's home, Luca could feel the questions playing in Valerie's mind. Secrets stood between them. For the first time in his life, he wanted to punch a hole right through that wall.

LESS THAN TEN MINUTES later they reached the car. After they were well on their way, Valerie spoke.

"I have some questions I'd like you to answer. Let's start with those brothers of yours Tso mentioned. Do you come from a big family?" she asked, knowing that there was a lot more to it than that.

"I have no brothers or sisters," he answered after a lengthy pause.

"Then he meant the Brotherhood of Warriors."

Luca said nothing.

"You *knew* what he meant," Valerie pressed. "What's more, you made sure he dropped the subject fast."

"Assuming that's true, what makes you think I'd want to talk about it now?" he asked, a wry smile touching the corners of his mouth.

She looked at him, then shook her head in frustration. "You take privacy to a whole new level."

"You already know all you need to know about me," he said, his voice impossibly low and sexy.

"We've shared something beautiful, but true closeness?" She shook her head. "You won't allow that to happen."

"Is that the woman or the detective speaking now?" Luca asked.

"Both are me," she said softly. "You, of all people, should understand that."

"I do," he said in a quiet voice.

Yet Luca still hadn't answered her initial question. "Okay, so tell me something else," she said. "What was that deal about Browning collecting *Deez's* trash?"

"One way a skinwalker works is by collecting samples of his victim's hair, nail clippings and other personal items. He uses those in his rituals—to witch them."

"And that blowpipe stuff?"

"Another method of witching. They can blow pieces of bone into you, or beads that are contaminated with something that'll make you sick or put a curse on you."

"Ugh."

"Is that GPS back on?" he asked her, glancing at the device now in the center console between them.

"You bet it is," Valerie answered. "Getting back to Browning... Do you think he's our man?"

"Stranger things have happened, I suppose," he said, looking in the rearview mirror on the passenger's side. "A reporter needs a story big enough to resurrect his career, so he decides to manufacture one."

"It's plausible, I know, but you know what? There's something about it that just doesn't feel right to me. Browning's a user and a manipulator, but something tells me he's not a killer."

"Maybe so, but I still believe he plays a part in all this," he said. "What we need to do now is talk to Dr. Becenti."

Valerie was about to agree when a call came through on the radio. Captain Harris wanted them in his office as soon as possible. Valerie gave him their ETA, then concluded the transmission.

Fifteen minutes later, they greeted Captain Harris's secretary, Michelle, then went into the captain's office. Luca studied the man before him. Although he was skilled at reading people, he saw nothing in Captain Harris's face.

Harris typed something into his computer, then angled the monitor display toward them. "The local paper ran a story revealing that you're trying to catch the killer by using the GPS he planted on you. The same story's running on the Internet. The 'Skinwalker Murders' are top news."

"So that game plan goes out the window now. Browning did hint that he had a contact in this department," she explained.

Captain Harris's eyes flashed with uncharacteristic anger. "I've got a leak in my department?"

Had his voice been loud, or unusually gruff, it would have packed far less power than that emotionless, arctic tone.

"Whoever gave him the story will soon be cleaning out their desk," Harris said.

Despite the determination in his voice, Luca doubted that the captain would get far. Things of this nature were often difficult to pinpoint, and reporters were notoriously careful to guard their sources. But the quality of life here at the station was about to take a drastic turn.

Harris walked across the room, shut the door to his office then returned to his seat. "I received a call earlier from Dr. Becenti, a professor at the college," he said. "He's asked to speak to the investigating officers. He says he's got some information on skinwalkers we may find helpful."

"He was next on our list of interviews. We'll go pay him a visit," Valerie said.

"Good. Get to it." They turned toward the door, then Harris spoke again. "One more thing I forgot to mention. Tests on those human bones are coming in, and there's some Y chromosome mumbo jumbo that answers at least one question."

Valerie and Luca, curious, both turned to face the captain.

"The bones came from a member of my tribe?" Luca asked, following his gut instinct.

"Right. Everything keeps pointing back to the Navajo connection," Harris answered.

"So the bones may have come from a Navajo cemetery. And both college professors have spent time on the reservation in recent months," Valerie added. "All the more reason to speak to Becenti."

Luca closed the door behind them on their way out, nodded to Captain Harris's young office assistant but said nothing until they were well down the hall. "Whether he's a grave robber or not remains to be seen. But Becenti suffered a major loss of face after his last visit to the Navajo Nation. He may see this case as a chance to recover some of the ground he lost when Dr. Finley upstaged him. I'd lay odds he'll volunteer to become a consultant for the police."

"I hate consultants and experts," Valerie muttered under her breath.

"You must not have been too thrilled when I came on the scene," he answered.

"I wasn't, but lately you've gone to great lengths to prove me wrong on that. And your efforts have been…impressive," she added with a smile.

The mischievous spark in her eyes and the playful challenge in her voice started a fire inside him. Valerie Jonas could stir his blood without even trying. Luca took a deep breath, and glanced away from her.

A woman like Valerie deserved more than he could give her. He was bound to his duty, and the Rez was his home. Valerie had made a place for herself here, and she needed those roots she'd worked hard to establish.

What he could offer her would take away more than it would give. His path in life was set. He would continue to honor his alliance to the Brotherhood and his work restoring order and bringing harmony to his tribe.

Last night had been a celebration of life. He'd carry that memory with him for as long as he lived. But everything had two sides and for every measure of joy they'd found in those stolen hours they'd soon discover an equal, if not greater, amount of pain.

Chapter Eighteen

They were walking across campus, cutting through the big lawn west of the main library, when Valerie finally broke the heavy silence that had once again stretched out between them.

"You're just not a great conversationalist, are you?"

"Are you kidding? I'm a regular motormouth," Luca answered without cracking a smile.

She laughed. "I'm not even going to ask if that's what you think I am." The ringing cell phone interrupted her. After listening for a moment she hung up. "Apparently, Dr. Becenti's done a lot of work on the Rez over the years," she said, giving him the results of the background check. "Think about it for a moment. Does his name sound familiar to you at all?"

"The Rez is a very large place, covering parts of three states. I don't know every Navajo—or part Navajo—on our land, no more than you know everyone within, say, two hundred miles of downtown Albuquerque."

Valerie started to protest that she hadn't meant that at all, when she saw him give her one of his rare smiles. She realized, suddenly, that he'd been teasing. "I never know what to make of you."

"Would you prefer someone more predictable?"

She wouldn't have changed one thing about him, but no way was she going to tell him that. Instead, she let out a belabored sigh. "You're just one of those guys who's put on this earth to test women."

"Test them? How?" he asked. "True or false, matching, multiple choice, essay?"

Valerie raised her eyebrows. "I guess you'll have to figure that one out yourself. I don't want to give you all the answers. You have too many of them already."

"Answers? I haven't got any answers," he replied, now realizing she hadn't been teasing. "What on earth are *you* talking about?"

Liking the fact that he couldn't figure her out anymore than she could him, she smiled. "See that? There's balance between us. I can't get a bead on you and you can't figure me out either."

Luca shook his head.

As they entered the building, Valerie asked for directions from a passing student, and soon thereafter they arrived at Dr. Becenti's office.

Valerie and Luca identified themselves as they went inside the small, crowded room, but it was Dr. Becenti's reaction to Luca that intrigued Valerie the most. As a woman, she was used to getting men's attention when she walked into a room. Yet the professor had scarcely glanced at her. His attention was focused solely on Luca.

"Tribal Police…" Dr. Becenti repeated thoughtfully as they identified themselves. "I would have thought sending a *hataalii* would have been more appropriate."

"Homicides are under the jurisdiction of the police, Professor. I'm here to help county law enforcement with their investigation because I have some knowledge of the practices this killer's using."

"I'm one-fourth Navajo and my doctorate is in cultural anthropology," Dr. Becenti said. "I specialize in the *Diné* so I'd like to offer my expertise to the department as well," he said, looking at Valerie now. "I've studied the ways of the skinwalkers extensively. Do you know much about them?" he asked, looking over at Luca.

Luca was tempted to direct the professor not to use the word so casually but somehow he refrained. Instead he shrugged, noting that if Becenti had a medicine pouch, it was out of sight.

"I suppose it's hard to learn about something that's rarely spoken about aloud," Dr. Becenti said in a much more animated tone when Luca failed to answer. "But my knowledge is at your disposal. I understand from one of the newspaper articles that the killer has cut fingers off each of the victims. Do you know why that is?"

"Souvenirs," Valerie said flatly. "It's not at all unusual for a serial killer to collect something from his victims. There may also be personal items missing we don't know about—yet."

"But you're not up against an ordinary serial killer, Detective," Becenti said in an arrogant tone. "You see? That's why I could be of help to you on this case. Few have the specialized knowledge I've acquired on this subject over the years."

"Be careful, Professor. We might start looking at you as a suspect," Valerie said, only half-jokingly.

"Amusing, but with all the classes I teach, my whereabouts, even after hours, are pretty well established," he answered. "But we're getting sidetracked. Do you know why he took the fingers?" He glanced at each of them then continued, "Navajo ways teach that life enters the body through the ears. When death claims it, life goes out through the fingers. Some believe that fingerprints—the whorls in our fingers—are the physical imprint left behind by the first spirit ever freed from its body by death."

Luca nodded, having known the answer since he was six years old. The fact that the professor also had known about this attested to the extent of the man's knowledge—or careful research.

"The fact that the killer's utilizing little-known facts like those tells me you're dealing with the real thing—a genuine skinwalker," Becenti said, his voice rising an octave with excitement.

"And that's why you're so interested?" Valerie asked.

"Of course. Even if this person has none of the supernatural powers accorded to skinwalkers, his body of knowledge is still impressive. I'm a university professor, always in search of answers. After you catch this—individual—I intend to do my best to interview him at length."

As he detailed his plans, Luca surveyed Dr. Becenti's office, studying the contents of the shelves and walls. There were Indian crafts all around the room as well as Hispanic works of art. "You like all of the Southwestern culture, not just that of the Navajo."

Dr. Becenti nodded. "We live in one of the most culturally diverse areas of the United States. Providing you keep an open mind, there's no limit to what you can learn about our neighbors, past and present."

Luca noted collections on *brujería* and voodoo, but it was one leather-bound book by a Navajo author that immediately caught his attention. It contained the memoirs of an Anglo woman who'd married a renowned medicine man.

Dr. Becenti came over and stood behind him. "That's an interesting volume," he said quietly. "It speaks of a secret organization on the reservation, the Brotherhood of Warriors. I believe the group exists to this day but I haven't been able to document any of its history or practices. I traveled into the heart of the Rez last summer to conduct my research, but I got nowhere, even with Navajo blood flowing through my veins…."

"If it's a secret organization, maybe they wanted to keep it that way," Luca said. "But traveling across the *Dinétah* is a wonderful way to spend the summer, and all it cost you was a little gas money, right?"

"More than that." Becenti's eyes flashed with anger, but when he spoke his tone revealed no traces of it. "I had to return my grant money, and it created a few other…misunderstandings." He turned away from Luca and returned to his desk. "But it's all water under the bridge now."

Valerie cleared her throat, then diplomatically brought him back on target. "I understand that you had some specific information you wanted to share with us."

His expression grew grave and he nodded. "Though the majority of my students are Navajo or part Navajo, there are some who come from other cultures. Currently there seems to be a healthy interest in the various American Indian tribes and their cultural practices." He paused, looked at Luca then back at Valerie. "Have you considered the possibility that you might be dealing with an Anglo—someone desperate to belong to something—anything—that'll help define him, even if what he chooses is totally repugnant?"

"Do you have someone in mind?" Valerie asked him.

He nodded. "Two individuals, actually. First there's the reporter who's writing the series on the 'Skinwalker Murders.' We've spoken over the phone a few times and he seems very knowledgeable for an Anglo."

Valerie nodded. "We've met him. Who's the other?"

Becenti hesitated briefly then continued. "These are special circumstances. I don't think I'll be violating my professional obligations by letting you know about a *former* student of mine. His name is Frank Willie. He dropped out of my class last semester. He'd disagreed with the grade I'd given him on his research paper and went as far as to threaten me."

"Threaten you how?" Valerie asked.

"I'd been giving lectures on Navajo witchcraft practices, and when I came back to my office one night, I found a dry painting made with ashes on my desk. The figure in the center represented me, and he'd vandalized it in the way a skinwalker would have if he'd intended on making his victim go insane. When I hurried out of my office to see if anyone was around, I saw him at the end of the hall. He was standing there, laughing. Before I could say anything, he hurried out the door, and I didn't see him again—until yesterday."

"What happened yesterday?" Valerie asked.

"He was waiting for me here in my office. He wanted to get back into my class. He said that what he'd learned from me had empowered him. I have no idea what he meant by that, and I didn't ask. I just told him to get out."

"Did he leave right away?" Luca asked.

"No, not at first. After he realized that there was no way I'd ever let him even audit one of my classes, he finally left," he said. "But he was in a rage. He swore to make me pay."

"Did you confront him about the dry painting before he left?" Valerie asked.

"Not exactly. I just told him that leaving me souvenirs like those wouldn't get him what he wanted. Skinwalker practices can engender fear, but only if you believe in that sort of thing."

"And you don't?"

He hesitated. "I've never seen real supernatural power. If I did, I might fear it. But until I do…" he said, then shrugged.

"I'll need the student's address and a description," Valerie said.

Becenti handed her a small piece of paper from a notepad that was under the paperweight on his desk. It contained the student's social security number, student number and his physical description. "That's everything I've got on Frank Willie. There's no phone number written down because he never gave us one, and records doesn't have a valid address."

"Thanks, Professor," Valerie said.

As they headed back across campus, Valerie glanced at Luca. "We've tried to track down Frank Willie before but his last address didn't pan out."

Luca nodded. "If I remember correctly, he lived with the second victim for some time."

"Maybe her friend Mae can give us a lead now that she's had time to think about things," Valerie said. "I should have the contact number for her here somewhere," she added, searching her PDA.

Valerie made the call and was lucky enough to catch Mae. A few minutes later, as they reached her vehicle, she hung up.

"I got some of that," Luca said, "including the fact that we now have an address on Frank Willie. Fill me in on the rest."

Valerie nodded. "It appears that Frank called Mae just before she and her father left home yesterday—not long after we left. According to Mae, Frank was upset and wanted to know where Lea was going to be buried so he could pay his respects. Mae didn't want to talk about it and told Frank to contact Lea's family directly. Frank said he'd tried but they'd hung up on him twice already."

"No surprise. No one would be eager to talk about the dead—particularly to an old boyfriend they undoubtedly hadn't approved of," Luca said.

"According to Mae, he'd seemed genuinely upset by the news of her death," Valerie said, climbing in and unlocking his door from the inside.

"If he'd cared for the woman at one time, and I'm assuming that's the case, news of her death could have affected him deeply. Something like that can blast a hole through a man no matter how strong he is."

"You're not just speaking about him, are you?" Valerie asked in a gentle voice as she started the engine. "You had to deal with the death of a woman you cared about, too."

"Yes." Luca glanced at her, not surprised by how accurately she'd learned to read him. Wanting her to know—and maybe understand—why there was no place for love in his life, he continued. "She was helping my dad deliver hay to stranded livestock following an unexpected snowstorm. Normally that would have been my job, but I was halfway across the Rez working on a case, so she decided to help me out." He paused for several seconds. "Early that morning her truck slid off an icy road and overturned. By the time my dad found her, she was dead."

"I'm so sorry." Although her heart went out to him, she could sense he didn't want her sympathy. She waited, trying to understand what he was really trying to tell her.

"When she needed me most, I wasn't there. After that, I sank into darkness that poisoned me from the inside out." He grew silent for several moments. "The one thing I learned as I worked my way out of that hellhole is that some of us aren't meant for relationships.

"Police work carries a high price, but just as you have, I've accepted the demands of the job. As officers our duty's clear. Relationships—those are much more complicated."

"Yeah, I hear you."

A trace of sadness wound through her. They were perfect for each other. If anyone could understand Luca's passion for the work they did, it was her. But he'd closed the doors between them, just as she'd done, though for different reasons.

Growing up moving from neighborhood to neighborhood, school to school, never having anyone to call a friend—at least not for long—had taught her never to count on tomorrow. She'd lived life moment by moment and asked for nothing else. Then Luca had stepped into her life and made her question her most cherished beliefs. But to fall head over heels in love—to surrender to that volatile emotion—meant trusting in hope, the kind that defied the odds, and she'd seen too much of life to do that.

"Believing in long-term relationships is as hard for me as believing in fairies with wings and wands," she admitted softly. Yet one thing *had* changed. Since she'd met Luca she'd found herself wishing she could.

"So, love is for others, not you?"

"Yes," she answered. "Love is expectations coupled with imagination, and that never fails to get people in trouble." Valerie told him about her mother's great quest to find her one true love.

"Fantasies and reality don't mix," he said. "Life is far more than that."

Valerie glanced over at him. As illogical as it was, Luca was precisely the kind of man she'd always dreamed about deep in the night when darkness kept caution at bay. She'd wanted a warrior, a man who'd stand by her no matter what the danger, and someone confident enough to be capable of exquisite tenderness.

Angry with herself for allowing her thoughts to stray, she swept those feelings aside. Luca was her partner and he'd be leaving just as soon as they'd made an arrest. She wouldn't spend another second wishing for something that could never be. Besides, she wasn't cut out for domesticity. Her life was fine just the way it was.

Valerie kept her eyes on the road, and, following the output from the navigation system display, reached Frank Willie's new address. Sticking to her training, Valerie parked down the street. The old twenties-era brick building was a few miles north of downtown Albuquerque. Most of the former family homes here had been converted to businesses and now housed bail bondsmen operations, offices or realty firms. The few that still survived as residences had been turned into apartments or duplexes.

Frank Willie's front door opened as they climbed out of the car. A man who fit his description walked to the sidewalk carrying a black plastic trash bag and dropped it into the waste bin at the curb. As he turned, he looked directly at them then casually began walking in the opposite direction.

"Stop where you are. I'm Detective Valerie Jonas of the Sheriff's Department," she called out.

Willie took off like a shot.

"We've got a runner," Valerie said to Luca. "Let's go."

Chapter Nineteen

Willie cut across a legal firm's front lawn and raced into the alley behind the building, disappearing from view. Luca pursued, quickly outdistancing Valérie.

Willie soon reached the end of the block and sprinted alongside a big wooden fence at the back of an apartment. Seeing Luca behind him, he ran out into the cross street, forcing oncoming cars to brake hard or swerve to avoid hitting him.

Luca was forced to stop for oncoming cars as he reached the end of the alley, and Valerie caught up to him. "More officers are closing in to back us up. He's not going anywhere," she said, crossing the street with him.

Resuming the chase down the sidewalk, they could see Willie running half a block ahead, now approaching a tall, old brick building, probably a warehouse. A crowd of people filled the sidewalk, then split into two lines leading up the steps to the building. A tall fabric sign hung above the door advertised job interviews at the nationally known electronics firm.

Willie plunged into the crowd of mostly young people, shoving and pushing his way through until he disappeared from view.

Luca and Valerie tried to follow, but found their way blocked by a crowd that had been angered by Willie's aggressive intrusion.

"Back of the line," one woman yelled.

Sidestepping her, Luca jumped up onto the concrete railing of the stairway. From that vantage point he could see the top of Frank Willie's head as he shoved his way along the crowded sidewalk. It was like swimming upstream through a debris-filled creek.

Luca watched people react to him, then saw the top of Willie's head as it disappeared to the left, around the corner of the building.

Luca yelled to Valerie, who was inching her way along, holding her badge in front of her like a cattle prod. "He turned left at the corner," he called out. "I'm circling around to the east."

Luca jumped down then ran around the side of the building and entered the alley at the rear of the structure. Except for the parked cars he had the route to himself and he reached the next cross street within seconds.

Luca stopped, wondering how far Willie had gone. He couldn't use footprints to track a suspect on a city street or sidewalk, but there were other signs—if you knew how to read them.

Brakes suddenly squealed about half a block east and he heard a crash. Betting that was a sign, Luca raced down the sidewalk. When he reached the corner, he saw a yellow taxi up on the sidewalk and a bent-over parking meter wedged beneath the vehicle's heavy front bumper.

"Which way did he go?" Luca asked the cab driver, who was still cursing as he stared down at the damage to his vehicle. Cabs were a rare sight to Luca, who couldn't recall ever having seen one on the West Virginia–sized Navajo Nation.

"Wild-eyed fool cut right out in front of me. He ran down that alley!" The cabbie pointed. "You a cop?"

"Yeah, call it in for me while I go catch the guy," Luca said, then took off across the street. The light had changed, and cars were stalled with the cab now blocking a lane. Luca was halfway down the block when he spotted Willie, who was still running as if he had a bear on his heels.

Studying the direction he was traveling, Luca smiled slowly.

"I've got you now, Mr. Willie," he muttered, taking out the cell phone. Punching in Valerie's number, he reached her instantly.

"What's your twenty?" she asked, wanting his location.

He turned and looked at the street signs. "Second and Commerce, but I've just figured out where he's going. He's headed back home via the alley between Second and Third. I'll follow on the west side of Second. You can head north, then just wait by the side of his house until he shows up."

"Meet you at the north end of his house," she said, then ended the call.

Luca jogged up the sidewalk, passing dozens of people along the way. Most didn't make eye contact—the way of the city and, strangely enough, the way of the Navajos.

Five minutes later, coming up the alley, he spotted Valerie in the shadows, barely visible, standing against the side of the building opposite Willie's home. Seeing him, she stepped out into his line of sight and shrugged.

Luca walked in her direction, checking the back doors of the buildings as he passed. Reaching an old garage, he noted a padlock on the ground just below where the two doors were joined. An empty hasp was open. He gestured, pointing to his eyes then at the lock, showing her where to look.

Valerie saw the lock, which had been opened with a key, and understood what he was suggesting. She took a position beside one door and brought out her pistol, ready to back him up.

Luca jerked open the door by the handle. Willie, who'd been holding the door from the inside, was suddenly yanked out into the alley, a wrecking bar in his hand. In a panic, he took a swipe at Valerie's pistol, but she just stepped back, easily avoiding the clumsy attempt.

"Drop it, Willie!" she ordered.

Willie took another swing anyway, forcing her to step back again.

"I don't want to have to shoot, but one more swing and I'll do it. Now drop the weapon," she ordered.

Luca came in from the side and knocked Willie's feet out

from beneath him with a leg sweep. The man fell down hard, dropping the wrecking bar.

Still refusing to give up, Frank made a desperate grab for the big tool. Valerie stepped down hard on his wrist and held her fist against his windpipe. "Give it up," she said. "Roll over, facedown."

"Okay, okay," he managed, completely out of breath.

After Valerie took her foot off Willie's wrist and moved her hand away, Frank rolled over onto his stomach and Luca applied handcuffs.

"You're under arrest for murder, Frank Willie," Valerie said.

"*Murder?* You're out of your mind."

Luca opened the garage door and looked inside. "I'll be willing to bet most, if not all, of this stuff's hot," he said, glancing back at Willie.

"Yeah, yeah, and it has my prints. So you've got me for burglary. But no way you're pinning any murder on me. I'd never hurt Lea or that other woman."

"Convince me," Valerie snapped.

"I've heard the news. When the first woman was killed, I was cooling my heels in jail. I'd had a disagreement with another guy playing blackjack at the casino."

"We'll check it out, so you better not be lying to me. I really dislike people who waste my time," Valerie said, purposely biting off every word.

As another officer came up to take custody of Willie, a call came over Valerie's radio. Hearing the code for a ten-twenty-seven-one, a homicide, Valerie moved away from Luca and the police officer.

After getting all the pertinent information, she joined Luca. "We've got to move. Another body's been discovered, and it looks like the same M.O."

As they hurried back to her unit, Valerie filled him in on what she knew. "Some hikers came across the body of a Navajo woman in her early twenties. The body's near a campground in the Manzanos about ten miles south of Tijeras. According to the deputy on the scene, her fingers have been cut off. The rest of the M.O. also matches our perp's work. But there's something new this time." She swallowed, determined to keep her voice steady. "A photo of you and me was left by the body."

"Where was the photo taken?"

"I don't know yet. I figured we'd see for ourselves once we got there," Valerie said.

They reached I-25 via Central Avenue, drove north to the Big I then raced east out of the city on I-40. With emergency lights flashing they made very good time, and twenty-five minutes later they were in what locals called the Canyon. From there, they turned south, taking the same route at first that they'd followed to the Nez home.

Ten minutes later they arrived on the scene, a small meadow within a hundred yards of a camping-area picnic table. Three Sheriff's Department cruisers were already there, along with the mobile crime lab, and the scene had been cordoned off with yellow tape.

As she got out, one of the older, more experienced deputies greeted her with a grim nod. "Hold on to your stomach, Jonas. It ain't pretty," he muttered.

"Do you have an ID?"

"Yeah, I recognized her…name's Elaine Bowman."

"Navajo?" Valerie asked.

"Yeah."

"How do you know her?" Valerie asked, curious why the vic had been recognized.

"I'm taking an afternoon class at the U. She operates a hot dog stand on the north side of Central right in front of old Johnson Gym. She's got—had—the best hot dogs in the city."

Valerie nodded, having seen the cart a few times while on campus. There were not that many sidewalk hot dog vendors in their city, and the university area was a good place for her kind of business. She was an original.

Putting on their latex gloves, they approached the scene and ducked under the yellow tape. She'd seen the two other bodies but this one was worse. She swallowed. Blood completely covered the victim who had multiple stab wounds on her chest.

"She put up a fight," Valerie said.

"That might have made things worse for her," Luca said in a quiet voice.

"Worse than dead? I would have done the same thing in her shoes—do my best to take a piece of him with me," she said.

He nodded in approval. It was Valerie's fighting spirit that drew him most. Merilyn had needed, and wanted, to be taken care of, but Valerie demanded something different from a man—the right to coexist in his world. That didn't make her less of a woman, just one whose needs he understood.

"Once she stopped struggling, the killer took his time with her," he said. Crouching next to the victim, he studied the intricacy of the ash painting beside her. He then gazed at her bloody forearms, immediately recognizing the insignia carved into her flesh—flames bounded by a circle—the sign of the Brotherhood.

"Here's the photo," Valerie said, interrupting his thoughts. "It's attached with some kind of weird arrowhead to the rubber sole of her right shoe."

He came up behind Valerie. "That's a bone arrowhead."

"Piercing *my* head in the photo," she muttered, remembering their talk with Dr. Becenti. "This photo of us was taken *after* we came back from the mountains and went to the station. We took a break and went across the street for some coffee while we waited for the fingerprint check on the tracker, remember?"

"Yeah," he answered, still focused on the arrowhead. "We'll need to know where the bone used for the arrowhead came from—an animal or human," he clarified, then pushed open the victim's purse. It lay beside the body, the catch unfastened. "Look at what I just found."

"Steve Browning's business card," Valerie noted. "You and I should go pay him a visit. Curiously enough, he *didn't* beat us to this crime scene."

"Do you think he's the killer and has been playing us all along?" Luca asked.

Valerie shook her head. "He wouldn't have left his card for us to find if he were. He's not stupid. Either way, we're going to bring him in for questioning. I want to sweat some answers from him. He's been holding out on us all along and that's got to stop."

"The press…"

"Yeah, I know. We'll tread carefully. But this woman had rights, too."

Walking back to the car, Valerie remained silent. As she slipped into the driver's seat, she gripped the steering wheel hard, trying to hide the way her hands were shaking.

Aware of it, Luca reached across and brushed her cheek with his knuckles. "Ease up. It's all right," he said, his voice low and deep.

"We should have had this killer behind bars by now. Instead, he's playing mind games with us."

"We're closing in on him and that's why he's playing with us. He wants to mess up our thinking."

Frustration ripped through her. She liked battles that were more out in the open, but everything in this case was shrouded in layers of secrecy.

"Just know that you're not in this fight alone. You're a strong woman who can handle herself, but it never hurts to have backup." Luca took her hand and wove his fingers through hers.

The gentleness of his touch swept past her defenses. His strength was unassuming yet as solid as the mountains that loomed above them.

She'd spent her entire life proving that she could stand alone. Yet a part of her still yearned to be protected—even as she protected others. She'd branded that instinct her most powerful enemy, but for the first time in her life she was ready to honor that softer side of her heart. True strength came in many guises.

Chapter Twenty

Valerie phoned Browning and got him on the first ring. From the tone of her voice and her side of the brief conversation, Luca knew that his instincts had been right on the mark. Trouble—it wasn't far from them now.

Valerie closed the phone, stuck it in her shirt pocket then glanced over as they got underway. "Browning's at home, scared out of his mind. He's convinced he's the evil one's next target because of something he's uncovered. But he won't tell me anymore until we get there. He wants us to come over ASAP."

"Do you think he knows the identity of the killer?"

She shook her head. "I think he would have said so if he knew for sure just to take the bull's-eye off himself. It's more likely that he's uncovered a lead to the killer's identity and now he's terrified. He said he's going to write up his story this afternoon. It'll run in tomorrow's morning edition, but between now and then he's got to stay alive—his words, not mine."

The interstate helped shorten their travel time, but it still took them forty minutes to reach the road that led to Browning's home. He lived out in the country, west of the adjacent city of Rio Rancho. The narrow dirt road crossing the desert plateau was filled with so many dips she had to cut her speed. Even so, they left a trail of dust that was visible for miles.

They'd just turned onto the gravel track leading to his house when they heard two shots in rapid succession. She pressed down on the gas, then slid to a stop beside a sandstone bluff fifty yards from the modest flat-roofed stucco dwelling.

Pistols in hand, they left the car, moving forward in a crouch, but there were no further shots. Using the few places that provided concealment to their advantage, they advanced toward the house slowly, covering each other.

Once at the open front gate, they slipped through, then circled around to the rear of the home, suspecting that would be the access of choice for an intruder. As they reached the rear corner of the house, Valerie did a quick visual search of the backyard. A small metal storage shed was in the far corner and there were tumbleweeds growing in a low spot. The rear door of the house was open, swinging slightly in the breeze. Valerie inched along the wall and peered inside but saw no one.

"Browning!" she called out. There was no answer.

"I'm going in. Cover me," she said.

"Wait." Luca grabbed her shoulder and stood rock still, listening. A weak, yet familiar voice was calling out to them.

Noticing a trail of blood leading to the shed, Luca broke into a run. "Call the paramedics!"

"Police," he announced as he arrived, his back pressed up against the wall of the metal shed. The door was open about an inch.

"Guys, I'm here," an unsteady voice called out.

Browning was huddled behind some bags of potting soil in the far corner and bleeding from a gunshot wound to his side. He had a dishcloth pressed against the wound, which had apparently stemmed the flow somewhat. When Luca drew near he could see that the man had lost a lot of blood.

"Who did this to you?" Luca asked, crouching beside Browning, weapon still in hand.

"Skinwalker," he managed. He drew in a shaky breath. "He came to the house…shot me through the living room window. Must have circled around from the back…"

While Valerie watched, Luca did what he could to help the

man, fastening the makeshift bandage in place with some duct tape he found on a small shelf.

As Valerie moved away, maintaining contact with the dispatcher on her cell phone, Luca noticed that Browning's breathing was becoming shallower. It was clear he was fighting to stay conscious.

"He's doing all this to challenge the Brotherhood," Browning whispered. "He hates them, blames them for spreading lies about him. They…" Browning's voice slowly faded away.

Luca checked Browning's pulse. The man was alive but unconscious.

"Is there an ETA on the medics?" Luca said.

"Five minutes," Valerie said, off the phone now and striding quickly toward the house. "I'm going inside. Maybe we can find something better to use as a bandage," she said. "Stay with Browning."

As he stood, Luca caught a whiff of something that got his immediate attention—fumes, like from a gas heater.

"No! Stay away from the house!" he yelled.

Hearing a loud pop, Luca dove and knocked her to the ground. A powerful wave of heat blew over them as the earth shook, and they were deafened by the blast from the explosion. His back and legs were showered with debris, cutting and tearing into his skin, but Valerie was beneath him, protected.

Heavy objects impacted all around them, then came a shower of shattered wood, roofing tiles and the rattle of thousands of objects as they descended back to ground.

Luca turned to look. The house, now less than a third the height as a moment earlier, was engulfed in flames and he was intensely aware of the heat and smoke.

"You're on fire!" Valerie shouted.

She scrambled to her feet, brushing the glowing embers off his back, then yanked the shredded fabric off him, tearing away his shirt.

Needing to put more distance between them and the house, Luca grabbed her hand and ran with her back to the shed. The shock wave had slammed into the tiny building with great force and it was now leaning to one side. A section of its metal roof had caved in about a foot after being hit with what looked like a piece of the kitchen sink.

They checked on Browning, and the side of the shed was still intact. His breathing, though shallow, remained steady.

Valerie glanced back at what was left of the house. "Wow. His home—it's gone," she said, still gathering her wits.

"The skinwalker must have loosened a gas connection and made some kind of fuse," Luca said, then gestured to his right. "There's a trail of dust over there. He may have stayed around long enough to make certain the house went up. Let me go see if I can catch a glimpse of his car. I'm a faster runner than you. Stay with Browning until the medics arrive."

By the time he reached the top of the rise behind the house, the vehicle was long gone. As Luca headed back he saw that a car, Browning's if he recalled correctly, was parked on the road. Perhaps the reporter hadn't wanted anyone to know he was home. The diversion obviously hadn't worked.

As he drew near, Luca studied the ground. There was only one set of prints around the car and he suspected they'd match the boots Browning had been wearing. Searching even more carefully beyond the vehicle, Luca picked up the faint signs of another's passage.

The skinwalker's skill was evident here. He'd hidden his tracks by walking atop tufts of grass or stones whenever possible. In the few places where he'd had to cross bare ground, he'd obscured his trail by sprinkling sand over his footprints.

Luca concentrated on spotting what was out of place. That was the only way to track someone this skilled. He found where his enemy had parked, but even here the trail was nearly impossible to discern. The killer had taken care to park on hard ground.

By the time he returned to Valerie and Browning, the paramedics had arrived. Working quickly, they'd stabilized the wounded man, then loaded him into their unit.

Valerie and Luca stood together as the ambulance pulled away, sirens wailing.

"Browning's notes and whatever else he had in his home are gone now," Valerie said. Then, hearing another set of sirens off in the distance, she added, "If that's the fire department, they're way too late."

"I wish Browning could have told us the rest of his story, but from the looks of it, that's not going to happen anytime soon," Luca said.

"I've made arrangements to have an officer protecting Browning at the hospital," she said.

"That's good, but we need to go a step beyond that," Luca said. "A Navajo investigator should be present there, too. If the killer returns to finish the job, he may not be carrying a firearm. He could decide to use the weapons of a skinwalker instead."

As they walked around the burning building, keeping their distance from the heat, Valerie became aware of everything about Luca. Seeing his naked chest gleaming against the chaos of the flames brought back memories of last night. In those precious hours she'd discovered magic in her lover's touch. And afterward, resting her head against him and listening to the strong beat of his heart, she'd found a peace beyond imagining.

Now evil had once again gained the upper hand, and duty called to her. "I'll request that a Navajo deputy or APD officer be assigned to the hospital."

"We'll need more than a police officer who happens to be Navajo," Luca said. "This job will require someone who knows the evil one's tactics and is trained to counter them. We need someone with credentials…similar to mine."

"You're thinking we should get a member of the Brotherhood for the job, aren't you?" she asked him in a quiet voice.

He said nothing for an eternity. "I've never spoken about this to an outsider, but you're closer to me than my own heartbeat," Luca said softly. Then, cupping her face in his hands, he continued. "What I'm going to tell you is something that you'll have to keep secret for as long as you live. Will you agree to do that?"

"Yes." Valerie held her breath and waited. This was what she'd dreamed of, to draw closer to him in ways that went beyond the physical.

"What you've suspected is true. I'm part of the Brotherhood of Warriors. We work in the shadows and do what needs to be done."

"I'll never betray you," she whispered, her heart singing.

Before she could say anything else, he leaned down and kissed her, parting her lips slowly, and loving her in the way only he could.

As she ran her hands over his shoulders in a slow caress, his muscles tensed under her touch and she could feel him struggle to hold himself in check. She drew back slightly and met his gaze. "You've shown me miracles," she whispered in awe of the multilayered world of feelings and tradition he'd opened to her. "No Brotherhood legend could compete with the man you are."

"I'm no legend, just flesh and blood," he said, kissing her again. "There are many things I want to say to you, but this isn't our time," he said, letting her go and stepping back. "To stay alive we'll need to stay focused. It's our only chance. Afterward…"

The promise of that one word wrapped itself around her, awakening all those secret longings she'd spent a lifetime denying.

Before either could speak again, the fire truck arrived and the firemen began to work. "I'll arrange to have one of my brothers guard Browning at the hospital. He can back up whoever your department assigns," he said.

"Unless the person you've got in mind is also a police officer, there's no chance of that happening," Valerie warned.

He smiled. "You're underestimating the influence the Brotherhood of Warriors has. After I make my call, your department will probably get a request directly from the governor's office."

Her eyebrows rose. "That's some clout." Valerie walked back with him to the car. "The killer knows about the Brotherhood. Do you think he also knows you're part of them?"

"He might suspect, but he won't come after me directly. He'd much rather I see what he's capable of doing right under my nose. It's his way of telling the Brotherhood that he's in control—not us."

"Makes sense," she said with a nod. "Go ahead and do whatever you have to do to get things rolling," she said, turning for one last look at the burning remnants of Browning's home.

Using the cell phone he'd been loaned, Luca dialed then spoke in Navajo for several minutes. When he ended the call, he looked over at her and noted that her expression had become guarded.

"What are you thinking?" he asked.

"We come from two such different worlds," she said softly. "I never belonged anywhere until I became an officer, but you have the force, your tribe, your brothers...."

"You have the department, including the deputies and officers you've worked with for years—and you have me," he said. He drew closer to her, but, aware of the others nearby fighting the blaze, made no move to touch her. "We're not so different, you and I. We're both driven by a need to make a difference, to make things better and safer for everyone else. It's our dedication to that battle that drew us together."

"Destiny... My mother used to talk about things like that—and I used to think she was nuts," Valerie said with a sheepish smile.

"We've both learned new things. The Navajo Way teaches that only by coming together are a man and a woman complete. I never really understood that—until you became part of my life," he said, gently brushing the side of her face with his hand.

"What are you saying?" she whispered.

"Afterward," he answered.

Even as she tried to prepare herself and accept the inescapable fact that one day he'd leave to go back to his world, a spark of something that wouldn't die flickered within her. Recognizing it, Valerie clung to it, and for the first time in her life yielded to the power of hope.

THE HOUSE WAS NOTHING more than burning embers now, and the fire marshal and crime scene unit were standing by waiting to sift through what remained for clues.

After grabbing a police jacket from the back of Valerie's car, Luca took in the scene. "We never checked Browning's car. It's parked out back."

"Then let's go take a look," she said, letting him lead the way.

They soon found Browning's yellow sports car with its faculty parking sticker, and not wanting any more surprises, began with a visual search.

"Nothing beneath it," Luca said, after crawling out of the undercarriage.

"I've looked through the windows, too, and there are no signs of problems inside. The perp didn't break in and the notebooks and papers on the floor don't look like they've been recently disturbed. There's a fine layer of dust on them."

"Okay, let's see if we can open the door." Finding the car locked, Luca reached into his pocket. "Time to improvise."

He brought out a small key-like tool attached to a ring and opened the lock within a few seconds.

"Did you learn that little skill at the police academy or spy school?" she asked with a grin.

He laughed. "None of the above. You'd be surprised what a poor kid from the Rez learns growing up."

Luca searched through the stack of papers in the backseat while she opened the glove compartment, which wasn't locked. "There's nothing special here, just three parking permits for the anthro department and a small notepad," she said, then opened it. "He's got several names and phone numbers listed—and here's one I recognize. It belongs to Michelle, Captain Harris's secretary, but this isn't Harris's office number. I think it might be her cell number." She paused, then looked over at him. "I think we may have found the department's leak."

"You're thinking she gave Browning the information about the GPS?" Luca asked.

"That's what I'm guessing. And here's something even more interesting. Browning's got Becenti's office *and* home phone number."

"If we can get a look at phone records we can establish the level of contact between Browning and Becenti. He may have been Browning's Navajo source all along, not one of the university students as we'd originally thought," he said.

"So Becenti jumps to the top of our suspect list," Valerie said. "But we still can't rule out Finley. He also has the background and resources to have learned how to play the role of skinwalker convincingly."

"I tend to think Becenti's a more likely candidate, but maybe that's because I just don't like the guy," Luca said after a beat.

"Why? What is it about him that bothers you?"

He considered his answer. "It's like *Deez* said. Navajo ways are far more than an interesting body of knowledge to analyze for three hours of college credit. Did you know that we don't even have a word for religion in the Navajo language? Our spiritual beliefs are woven into our everyday lives and are inseparable from them."

Valerie considered everything they'd learned, and after a long thoughtful pause said, "Let's go to the college. We'll talk to Becenti's teaching assistant and some of his colleagues and get a feel for who Becenti is—the man behind the professor, that is. Then we'll take a closer look and see how good his alibi is for the time of the murders."

Chapter Twenty-One

Wanting to avoid Professor Becenti until they were ready for him, they checked his class schedule and found out that he'd be teaching for the next hour. They then proceeded to track down his teaching assistant, James Campos. The young man was a short, barrel-chested Indian with long black hair in a ponytail. To Luca, he looked like he was from one of the Pueblo tribes.

The basement publications and journals area was quiet, and hearing their approach, James glanced up. "Police officers, right? I saw your photos in the newspaper. You must be here about the murders," he said. "How can I help?"

"James Campos? I'm Detective Jonas of BCSO. This is Detective Nakai of the Navajo Tribal Police. We're actually here gathering additional information on the victims. Did you know any of them?"

"Not the first one, but the ones who followed, yes. I heard the news on the street about the latest victim, Elaine. She had the best hot dog stand in the city. Dr. Becenti and I were regular customers and we're sure going to miss her. Elaine was beautiful in a way that kind of snuck up on you. She always had a smile for her customers, too," he said. "I tried asking her out a few times but she always turned me down." His eyes suddenly grew wide. "Hey, I'm not a suspect, am I?"

Valerie shook her head. Based upon the individual they'd

encountered on earlier occasions, Campos was too short and heavy to fit the profile. "What we need from you, James, is information. What can you tell us about Dr. Becenti? Is he considered an authority in his field?"

"Whoa! Is Dr. B a suspect?"

"Actually, we're looking into his background because we may need to use him more extensively as a source," Valerie said, unwilling to reveal the real reason. "A background check is all part of that. Can you tell me what he does between lectures and office hours, and how he spends his free time?"

"I haven't got a clue. All I do is grade his tests and take care of some clerical stuff."

Luca looked at the journals scattered on the desk. "Does he publish a lot in professional journals?"

"Oh, yeah. That's not only a university requirement, it's a real biggie for him. Dr. Finley and him are always competing for professional recognition. They both want to be known as *the* authority on the Southwestern tribes. Becenti has the edge when it comes to Navajo religious practices—particularly witchcraft. Of course it doesn't hurt that he's part Navajo."

"Does he have a lot of sources?" Luca asked, though he couldn't see it. The People just didn't talk about that particular subject.

"I think most of his information comes from books and private journals he's collected over the years. He's spent a fortune on memoirs, in particular. Some of those are so fragile he won't let anyone even photocopy them for the library archives."

"Have you read any of his papers and articles?" Valerie asked.

He shook his head. "It's not my area. I'm a Tewa linguist. But don't tell Dr. B. I need the job."

"How can we find and access the journal articles Dr. Becenti's written?" Valerie asked, looking around at the shelves filled with bound reference materials.

"You can get help from Peggy at the circulation desk," he said, indicating a deathly pale, slender young woman with long black hair and a lot of silver facial jewelry. "But most of the professional journals can't be taken outside the building."

"Okay, thanks," Valerie said.

"If *you* ask," he said, looking at Luca and grinning, "she'll look it all up for you and even carry it to your table. She likes the warrior type."

Valerie turned away, trying not to burst out laughing.

Five minutes later, Luca and Valerie were seated at a study carrel at the end of a row of shelves, three bound anthropology journal collections in front of them.

"I don't know how accurate Becenti's information is, but these articles are interesting," Valerie said, skimming one. "This one mentions a prominent *hataalii* with your last name. Is this your dad?" she asked, showing him the passage.

He nodded. "I told you about him."

"Your dad made it clear that certain subjects aren't to be spoken about, but Dr. Becenti goes on quoting unnamed sources—informants, he calls them. He details the dry paintings used by the evil ones, and how they bewitch their targets by defacing the figure within the circle. That all matches what we've seen at the crime scenes."

"But it doesn't prove Becenti's our man. This journal article could have been read by almost anyone interested in the subject."

"True, but these are specialized journals with a limited distribution. I would imagine that their readership is composed of anthropologists and students. You don't just drop in to read this kind of stuff."

"That still isn't enough to tie Becenti to the crimes," Luca said. "But knowing that Becenti had a connection to victim number two and victim number three is a start."

Valerie nodded. "And he—Finley, too—also made various trips to the Navajo Nation—and maybe some grave sites there. Either could have dug up the human remains we've found."

"Becenti's in better physical shape and built like a runner, too."

"Finley made an enemy of victim number two. Maybe he's also a hot dog fan," Valerie countered.

"We should focus on Becenti," Luca insisted. "I've got a gut feeling about him."

Valerie considered it, then said, "Becenti's teaching a class right now. What do you say we go try and take a look inside his office—unofficially."

"You mean break in?"

"It wouldn't be breaking in if his door's opened."

They arrived five minutes later. Although Dr. Becenti's office was locked, the one beside his was open at the moment and, more important, unoccupied. The common plate glass wall both offices shared gave Valerie and Luca an unobstructed view of Becenti's work space. From where they stood, they could see photos and other personal mementos that hadn't been there before.

"He cleaned house before we came over last time," Valerie said. "I should have expected that."

Luca held up one hand, interrupting her. "In cases like this it's easy to second-guess yourself but that'll get us nowhere. We did our best with the information we had at the time. That's all that's possible."

"Yeah, you're right. Only hindsight's flawless."

"Check out the photo at the edge of his desk, left side next to the phone. Isn't that a photo of victim number two?" Luca asked.

She pressed her face against the glass, hoping for a clearer look. "It wasn't there last time we went to his office. I'd swear to that. But I can't tell who that is…."

Hearing footsteps, Valerie turned as a young woman in jeans and a knit short-sleeved shirt stepped into the office. She was carrying a tooled leather purse, the strap over her shoulder.

"Hi guys," she acknowledged with a smile as Valerie held out her badge and introduced herself and Luca. "I'm Barb Cook, Professor Hebert's teaching assistant. I've heard about those university-area women getting killed and you asking around the department. Did you come to see Dr.

Hebert? Or are you looking for Dr. Becenti? If so, he won't be back for another half hour or so. He's teaching a class right now."

Barb stood behind Valerie, looked toward Becenti's office and sighed loudly. "He got the larger office, though we need the space more. Professor Hebert teaches field archaeology and has ten times as many students. We're bursting at the seams here. Maybe when Dr. H.'s next journal article comes out in the *Anthropology Review* he'll move up in the pecking order."

"Who's the woman in the photo?" Valerie asked casually, pointing. "Do you know?"

"That's his second cousin. They were close friends. She's full Navajo and lived back on the Rez. She died many years ago—a horseback-riding accident. Dr. Becenti was with her at the time, and I understand that he took her death really hard."

"Did *he* tell you that?" Luca asked, wanting to verify her source.

"No, Kay Porter filled me in. She and I were close last semester when she was Dr. Becenti's TA. But Kay had to drop out of school—family problems."

"Does Kay live here in town?"

Barb nodded. "Not that far from campus, actually, over near Roosevelt Park."

"We'll need her full address," Valerie said.

"Why? Do you think she could be involved in these crimes? She'd never hurt anyone," Barb said, immediately defending her friend. Then suddenly Barb stopped speaking and her eyes grew wide. "Wait a minute. You don't think *she* could be the next target, do you?"

"She's not in trouble, or in danger, that we know of. We're just trying to learn more about Professor Becenti," Valerie said, repeating her cover story. "And we'd appreciate it if you didn't mention our visit to Dr. Becenti."

"No problem. I avoid him whenever possible. That man could give anyone the creeps. He's so into all that witchcraft stuff."

Barb wrote down Kay's address and handed it to her. "Here

you go. Kay will be happy to help you. Truth is, by the time she quit she couldn't wait to get away from Becenti."

"Was it because of his obsession with witchcraft or something more?" Luca asked.

"The witchcraft stuff was part of it, sure, but there was more to it than that. Becenti's got one heck of a chip on his shoulder, and thinks he's far more important than he is. Even Dr. Finley, the department head, can't stand him. Those two disagree on everything. I've overheard some of their arguments—the ones coming from next door, at least."

"What do they argue about?" Luca asked.

"Scheduling, assignments and academic issues mostly. One time he and Finley really went at it over the class hours Becenti got assigned. Becenti wanted to know why he got all the odd hours." Her lips twitched and she added, "Finley told him that it fit him to a tee."

Luca and Valerie left the building shortly afterward. "Finley's still not off the hook completely, but I think you're right. We need to focus on Becenti," Valerie said.

"Let's go talk to his former assistant. After that, we'll have a better idea of what needs to be done next."

Chapter Twenty-Two

They were seated inside Kay Porter's small apartment ten minutes later. She was a slight, Anglo woman, older than either of them had expected. In her early sixties, she had a quiet dignity about her.

"You thought I'd be younger," Kay said with a smile, reading them accurately.

"Yes, but that was mostly because we've heard that Dr. Becenti has…shall we say, specific tastes?" Valerie said, taking a shot in the dark.

"Young Native American women? You're right about that. I think the only reason I got the job was because I'd met George three years ago on a dig. Back then, he found me easy to talk to," she explained. "Last year when I decided to work on my doctorate, I discovered I'd need extra income for tuition so I went to him. It only took a few days to realize how much he'd changed since we'd first met."

"In what ways had he changed?" Valerie asked.

"What used to motivate George was his desire to learn more about his culture. It wasn't making a name for himself," she said in a slow, thoughtful voice. "Back then, his curiosity came from the right place, if you get my meaning. He was particularly interested in *hataaliis,* though he certainly didn't have much respect for them."

"Did he ever tell you why?" Valerie asked.

"Only in bits, but I managed to piece it together. When he was just out of grad school, George apparently decided to track down all his distant relatives on the Rez. He located a few, but the only one who'd have anything to do with him was a distant cousin—a woman. One day they went out horseback riding and there was an accident. By the time George managed to get help, she'd passed away."

Even before she'd said anything more, Luca guessed most of the story.

"One of the woman's relatives was a *hataalii* who hadn't trusted George's motives from the beginning," Kay continued. "Then after the accident, rumors began circulating that George had become a skinwalker—killing a relative is one way a skinwalker gets his power. George blamed the *hataalii* for starting those stories. Then the *hataalii* passed away and, though the man died of natural causes, things got even worse for George."

"No wonder he had trouble getting anyone on the Rez to trust him," Luca said, understanding much more now.

"No one in the Arizona side of the Rez would even talk to him. Word continued to spread, and it soon didn't matter where he went—most of the *Diné* would refuse to have anything to do with him. He then changed tactics and started researching skinwalkers, something most Navajos won't talk about anyway. I'm guessing he got most of his information from old journals—or an actual skinwalker he managed to identify. Whatever the case, by the time he became a full professor, years later, he was considered one of the few authorities on that subject."

"Does he believe the rituals have power?" Luca asked.

"He doesn't like to admit it but I think he does. George told me once that the Anglo world is too quick to dismiss what it can't even begin to comprehend. He said he'd conducted experiments, and his results, though not conclusive, merited further study."

"Is it possible that his skinwalker studies corrupted him

and he eventually convinced himself he'd become what he was accused of being?" Luca asked.

"You think George is responsible for the murders?" Kay asked, suddenly horrified. "That doesn't sound like the man I worked with—not unless something happened to throw him off the deep end. I'd be more willing to believe that he knows who's been killing these young women and is keeping it a secret because he wants to study the crimes. But to actually go into the dark practices?" She shook her head. "George wants to make a name for himself. His ego demands it. That's why he wanted to devote one full semester to skinwalker practices and rituals."

"He actually taught that?" Luca said, taken aback.

"No. Finley threw the syllabus back into his face. Finley's a pioneer but he's also a realist. He knew a unit like that would create all kinds of flak in the community. Then the politicians would start circling in for the kill."

"How did Becenti take the news?" Valerie asked.

"At first he was furious. Then he changed his mind about the whole thing. He told me that teaching students about powers that could never be fully controlled was riskier than he'd realized. And before you ask, I have no idea what he meant by that."

"Do you know anything about his work on the Navajo Nation last summer?"

Kay nodded. "It was a mess. He found out that even though he was a full professor with impressive credentials, Navajos have long memories. The rumors about him had persisted all these years, and no one wanted anything to do with him. He came back empty-handed, but considering he's still teaching, I guess he recovered from that loss of face and moved on."

Valerie thanked the woman. As soon as Luca and she were alone in the car, she spoke. "Finley's not off the hook yet, but I disagree with Kay. I think Becenti's our man and your instincts were right on target all along." She expelled her breath in a hiss. "Now we need to prove it."

"The problem is that we have no hard evidence against either of those men," Luca said, then lapsed into a long thoughtful silence. After several minutes, he continued. "I think it's time for us to get creative."

"*No.* We need to go by the book," Valerie said. "Otherwise the case will be thrown out of court and a killer will walk. Creativity and police work don't mix."

"Agreed, but I have an idea that may work on all counts. It's clear that Becenti believes in the supernatural power the evil ones have. I say we use that against him—and his hatred for the Brotherhood."

"You've got my full attention now. What's your plan?"

"First, we'll need operatives who can keep both Finley and Becenti under surveillance."

"I can have a half dozen deputies assigned to us within the hour," Valerie said.

"We'll also need special Navajo operatives. First, we'll place wards around both Finley's and Becenti's offices and homes. Prayersticks, for example, and I think we should have the Coyote Prayer written in Navajo taped to their doors. Maybe we can even broadcast special chants sung by a *hataalii* over their cell phones. All these measures will convince the guilty one that other Navajos are wise to his true nature and are out to destroy him. Nothing is more dangerous to a skinwalker than being identified—and having his power rendered harmless."

"You want to mess with the minds of your suspects. I get it," she said.

"Then we'll get a female operative to pose as the *chindi*— the ghost of one of the victims—and goad him into taking further action."

"I'll do it. I'm not Navajo, but with makeup and a wig I can pull this off. He prefers to strike at night—we already know that—and anyone playing ghost will have to stay in the shadows to avoid too close an examination. That'll work to my advantage."

He felt as if he'd been punched in the gut. "I never intended for you—"

She held up one hand, interrupting him. "I won't pass the buck on this. Like you, I restore order—not by running from danger but by facing it squarely."

He gazed at her with undisguised admiration. As much as he would have preferred to keep her on the sidelines, he understood her need to stand up and be counted. "Then we'll see this through together."

As she saw herself reflected in his strong, steady gaze, Valerie felt completely understood. With Luca, she could be exactly who she was—an officer and a woman.

If only… Valerie suddenly turned away. Luca was everything she'd ever dreamed of, yet soon they'd have to say goodbye. She wanted to scream against the unfairness of it all. An aching sense of vulnerability that was totally unlike her swept over her. For the first time in her life she felt helpless. She desperately wanted to force Luca to need her—to *want* to stay…. But her world wasn't his, and she wasn't sure that there was a place for her in his life somewhere away on the reservation.

Although she'd told herself all along that memories would be enough, she knew differently now. Her heart would break and she'd never be the same again.

She swallowed hard. When the time came, even if that final goodbye took a piece of her heart and shattered it into a million pieces, she'd find the strength to do what had to be done.

Taking a deep steadying breath, she brought her thoughts back to the case. Work…for such a long time it had been at the center of her life. Now she realized that, by itself, it would never be enough.

Misinterpreting her silence, Luca asked, "Second thoughts?"

"None." She reached deep inside herself for courage. It was time to fulfill her duty. Brushing aside everything else for now, she became Detective Jonas once again. "It's time to put things into play. Where do we start?"

"I need to make a few phone calls."

IT TOOK SEVERAL HOURS to get everyone in place. Members of the Brotherhood and deputies of the Sheriff's Department had been deployed. Since the operation would begin on the university campus, the campus police had also been brought into play. The Albuquerque police department, which had city jurisdiction, was patrolling closely just outside the campus perimeter.

What normally would have taken days or weeks of red tape had been done in a matter of hours. As Luca had said, when the Brotherhood of Warriors got involved obstructions simply disappeared.

Valerie had taken great care with her makeup and clothing. Her disguise would fool just about anyone. She was about the same size as Lea Begay and was wearing clothing virtually identical to what the woman had worn on the night she'd been killed.

Originally, she'd hoped to wear the same bloodstained clothing found on the victim. Although she would have required permission to remove the items from the evidence locker, she'd been prepared to argue the point—until the Brotherhood members, and even Luca himself, had told her that they would refuse to work with her if she did that.

Standing before the mirror in the campus police station's restroom, Valerie carefully added the theatrical blood—borrowed from Albuquerque Studios—to the light-colored blouse and the jean jacket she was wearing, making sure the stain was directly over her heart. She'd already applied the realistic mix to the fabric at the center of her back. At a distance it would look like blood from the victim's fatal wound—a match with the crime scene photos. She'd also borrowed a phony finger with a gory, missing joint, from the special effects department of the movie and television production studio on Albuquerque's south side.

Valerie left the restroom, and met Luca in the office across the hall. He was dressed like a student, wearing sneakers, jeans, a loose-fitting jacket and carrying a book bag.

"Does it look real enough, you think?" she asked, turning around in a circle, then holding up her "wounded" hand.

Luca's lips were drawn thin. "Yes, it looks real—too much so."

"Then let's get to it," Valerie said, bracing herself for what lay ahead.

"You look…top heavy. I hope that means you're wearing the special ballistics vest," he said.

"Yeah, thanks to one of the female guards at the county jail."

"Good," he said. "Their vests provide better protection against edged weapons than our own. Regular law enforcement vests are great against bullets, but edged weapons can slip between the protective fibers." He clenched and unclenched his hand, then with a tightness to his voice, continued. "For this to work you may have to let the killer get within striking range when you whisper the word we taught you."

"*Yenaldlooshi*—skinwalker—I've got it," she said.

"Even if he realizes then that you're not Lea, he'll know he's been identified."

"I'll be ready."

"At the beginning, you'll be walking away from him, and your back will be to him. If he decides to attack before you actually turn and face him—"

"You'll stop him," she finished in a firm voice.

"The danger's still there," he said. "Let someone else do this," he added in a raw whisper.

She shook her head. "This is our job. If caring for each other means that we can't fulfill our duties anymore, we've sacrificed the best part of ourselves—what drew us to each other in the first place."

Accepting the truth didn't make things easier. Luca consoled himself with the fact that he'd be there to protect her every step of the way. No one would harm her—and live.

EVERYTHING had been meticulously planned. Since Becenti was the most likely suspect, they'd be concentrating on him first. If their role-playing trap didn't get a reaction from him, they'd move in on Finley, who was scheduled to be in the library until late with one of his study groups.

Becenti's last class of the day was held in Woodsman Hall, one of the older buildings southeast of the anthropology building. Plainclothes officers had been keeping watch on Becenti since he'd arrived on campus.

It was already 8:30 p.m. and getting darker by the minute. Information gathered from former students and instructional assistants had confirmed Becenti's routine. He stayed behind until all the students left, locked the classroom then walked to the faculty parking area and drove home.

The plan was for her to wait outside in the shadows until Becenti's class ended and he came out. Luca and the others were already in place along the planned route, ready to back her up in an instant.

Her phone vibrated and Valerie flinched. Cursing her nerves, she flipped open the phone. They'd decided not to use radios tonight because linking devices belonging to three departments and their various communications systems had proven problematic. Instead, all the major parties had been equipped with cell phones.

The caller was Roger, the campus officer who'd been placed inside the anthropology building. "Dr. Becenti just left his office."

"Acknowledged. Thanks," Valerie said.

Valerie took off the hot Windbreaker she'd worn and adjusted her jean jacket and light-colored blouse to give the fake blood—which retained a moist sheen—maximum impact. The next person to leave the building, if their plan went as expected, should be Dr. Becenti.

Valerie brought out her handgun, checking it one more time before returning it to her jacket. Fear was part of police work, but knowing Luca was out there, watching and guarding her back, bolstered her courage.

Valerie focused on the building before her. Seconds passed

with agonizing slowness. Finally she spotted Becenti coming out the double doors of the department's main building.

Here we go. She stepped over to the sidewalk and walked slowly away from the building, hearing Becenti's quick footsteps behind her as he narrowed the gap between them.

Not knowing if she was walking too fast or too slow, she continued down the sidewalk, crossing the big grass lawn that surrounded most of the campus structures.

She hated being a target facing the wrong direction. It went against all her instincts. Only the fact that she knew Luca had her covered kept her going.

As she neared the area where the darkness was the greatest—the spot where she'd be turning around to face the suspect—she braced herself. They'd know soon enough if Becenti was the skinwalker killer and a true believer in skinwalker magic.

As he was closing in on her position, she stepped partially out from the shadows. *"Yenaldlooshi,"* she said clearly.

Becenti stopped, startled. "Are you okay, miss?" he asked, trying to get a clear look at her despite the semidarkness.

Valerie repeated the word.

"Yes, that's what I teach, though your pronunciation leaves something to be desired," Becenti said matter-of-factly. "Come by my office tomorrow if you're interested in my classes. It's late now and I'm on my way home." Becenti walked past her, looking back over his shoulder once, then continuing on toward the parking lot.

Surprised, Valerie watched him go to his car, then drive out of the faculty lot and down the street.

Hearing footsteps behind her, Valerie turned and saw Luca jogging up. "In my mind I saw all kinds of scenarios playing out, but this one took me by surprise. Are you okay?"

Valerie nodded, her heart still hammering in her chest. "Yeah, I'm fine. I guess he's not the one."

"Or else he's playing it cool…. APD officers will follow him home then stake out his building."

"I better head over to the library so I can try this again with Finley," she said, as her heart rate returned to its normal rhythm.

"I'll walk you back," Luca said.

"No, you go ahead and get into position. If he comes out early and we're seen together, it could blow the plan."

As Luca walked away, Valerie made her way down the sidewalk toward the library, occasionally looking over her shoulder out of habit. Luca was still there watching over her. She could feel him close by. There was lighting in pools below each lamp but it was quite dark in other places, especially beneath the trees. She was near the corner of the old, western wing of the building when her cell phone vibrated again. She stopped, brought it out and from the number saw it was Roger, the campus cop.

"Detective Jonas," she said.

"Gotcha!" Becenti said, his voice coming from the telephone speaker—and from directly behind her.

Valerie whirled around to see Becenti in a hooded sweatshirt holding a bloodied hunting knife with a deadly looking curved blade. "You thought you could trick the Trickster, woman? I've already slit one throat tonight. Now let's see if you're any quicker than that campus cop."

Valerie kicked out, her foot catching Becenti's wrist and knocking the knife from his hand. As the knife flew into the air, Becenti cursed and reached for a small pistol in his waistband.

Suddenly Luca appeared out of the shadows, crashing into Becenti with a bone-shattering tackle. The two flew off the sidewalk onto the grass.

Valerie, her own pistol in hand, circled around the two men locked in battle, but it was too risky to shoot. When Becenti pressed his forearm over Luca's windpipe, she knew she had to do something fast.

"Kick him off, Luca, give me a clear shot!" she yelled, maneuvering for the right angle.

"I've got this—he's mine," Luca growled, breaking the hold in a burst of sheer strength.

Luca twisted free, punching his attacker in the gut and doubling him up. Becenti ducked his head and lunged, reaching for Luca's holster.

Luca grabbed his outstretched hand, twisted Becenti's arm around with a sickening crunch then chopped the man across the neck with the side of his hand.

Becenti groaned, then his body sagged to the ground, his eyes closing as he lost consciousness.

After cuffing Becenti, Luca's gaze instantly fastened on her. "Are you okay?" he asked, quickly drawing closer to her to see for himself. Fear had ripped into him when he'd seen Becenti threaten her with the knife. After that, all he'd felt was rage and the need to protect her at any cost.

"He didn't hurt me," she answered with a gentle smile. "Someone had my back."

"And I always will."

As other officers came running up, tears burned in her eyes. Their case had at long last come to a close. Luca and she had finished what they'd set out to do. Their future was now in the hands of destiny.

Chapter Twenty-Three

It was close to dawn by the time Valerie completed the pre-
liminary paperwork. The crime scene team was still sorting
though the damning "souvenirs" and other evidence, like
the snake capture stick the killer had hidden at his home.
She'd be adding their findings to her report later. At that time,
she'd also include the results of the interrogation still in
progress.

Browning was now in stable condition, and they'd have a
statement from him soon. The members of the Brotherhood,
along with the one who'd managed to render lifesaving first
aid to the campus cop, had long disappeared. She knew it was
only a matter of hours before Luca, too, returned to the world
he knew. While she'd been working, he'd packed up the gear
he'd left at the apartment and had brought his duffel bag to
the station.

"You've been avoiding me for the last few hours," Luca
said, coming up to her desk. "We have to talk."

The time she'd dreaded had finally arrived, but she
couldn't bring herself to say goodbye. "It's all this paperwork,
and you had to be debriefed—" She stopped and sighed.
"Yeah, okay, I confess. I just stink at goodbyes."

"We *need* to talk," he repeated, gesturing to the back door.

She couldn't bear to see him go. Already a huge lump had

formed at the back of her throat. "Just…do and say what you have to. I don't want to draw things out. It'll just make it worse."

"I'm not saying goodbye."

"I know, I hate that, too," Valerie answered. She would *not* cry. They were adults and they'd known this day would come. "This isn't really the end for us. We can call each other. Of course our careers will get in the way, but we might still find some weekend time together. Who knows? Maybe in a few months…"

Brushing aside her objections, he took her hand and led her outside to the old cottonwood that stood by the side of the station. As the moonlight filtered through its leaves, he cupped her face in his hands.

"What we've found is worth fighting for," he whispered, then took her mouth in an impossibly gentle kiss. *"Ayóó ninshné,"* he said, drawing back slightly to look at her.

"What does that mean?" she asked, suspecting the answer. "And after that bone-melting kiss, it better be 'I love you.'"

He laughed. "It is. I'll teach you other words later…as I show you what each means," he whispered in her ear.

A delicious shiver ran up her spine, but nothing could distract her from the one word he'd just spoken. "Later?"

Hearing the building door open and seeing Captain Harris coming their way, Valerie took a step away from Luca, hastily wiping a tear from her eye.

"Welcome to the department, Nakai," Captain Harris said, then walked past them toward his private parking slot.

Valerie looked back at Luca instantly, her heart in her throat. *"What* did he say?"

Luca smiled slowly. "I was just getting to that. I'm needed here. A lot of Native Americans live in and around the metro area, and someone who understands their special needs should handle cases that involve them. I brought the matter up with my brothers and, a few hours later, I was placed on permanent loan to this department."

She jumped into his arms. "I thought you were going home!"

"I already am. Wherever we're together, that's home," he said, pulling her against him.

With a contented sigh, she settled in his arms, her head resting over his heart.

* * * * *

*Celebrate Harlequin's 60th anniversary
with Harlequin® Superromance®
and the DIAMOND LEGACY miniseries!*

*Follow the stories of four cousins as they come to terms
with the complications of love and what it means to be a
family. Discover with them the sixty-year-old secret that
rocks not one but two families in…
A DAUGHTER'S TRUST by Tara Taylor Quinn.*

*Available in September 2009 from
Harlequin® Superromance®*

RICK'S APPOINTMENT with his attorney early Wednesday morning went only moderately better than his meeting with social services the day before. The prognosis wasn't great—but at least his attorney was going to file a motion for DNA testing. Just so Rick could petition to see the child…his sister's baby. The sister he didn't know he had until it was too late.

The rest of what his attorney said had been downhill from there.

Cell phone in hand before he'd even reached his Nitro, Rick punched in the speed dial number he'd programmed the day before.

Maybe foster parent Sue Bookman hadn't received his message. Or had lost his number. Maybe she didn't want to talk to him. At this point he didn't much care what she wanted.

"Hello?" She answered before the first ring was complete. And sounded breathless.

Young and breathless.

"Ms. Bookman?"

"Yes. This is Rick Kraynick, right?"

"Yes, ma'am."

"I recognized your number on caller ID," she said, her voice uneven, as though she was still engaged in whatever physical activity had her so breathless to begin with. "I'm sorry I didn't get back to you. I've been a little…distracted."

The words came in more disjointed spurts. Was she jogging?

"No problem," he said, when, in fact, he'd spent the better

part of the night before watching his phone. And fretting. "Did I get you at a bad time?"

"No worse than usual," she said, adding, "Better than some. So, how can I help?"

God, if only this could be so easy. He'd ask. She'd help. And life could go well. At least for one little person in his family.

It would be a first.

"Mr. Kraynick?"

"Yes. Sorry. I was…are you sure there isn't a better time to call?"

"I'm bouncing a baby, Mr. Kraynick. It's what I do."

"Is it Carrie?" he asked quickly, his pulse racing.

"How do you know Carrie?" She sounded defensive, which wouldn't do him any good.

"I'm her uncle," he explained, "her mother's—Christy's— older brother, and I know you have her."

"I can neither confirm nor deny your allegations, Mr. Kraynick. Please call social services." She rattled off the number.

"Wait!" he said, unable to hide his urgency. "Please," he said more calmly. "Just hear me out."

"How did you find me?"

"A friend of Christy's."

"I'm sorry I can't help you, Mr. Kraynick," she said softly. "This conversation is over."

"I grew up in foster care," he said, as though that gave him some special privilege. Some insider's edge.

"Then you know you shouldn't be calling me at all."

"Yes… But Carrie is my niece," he said. "I need to see her. To know that she's okay."

"You'll have to go through social services to arrange that."

"I'm sure you know it's not as easy as it sounds. I'm a single man with no real ties and I've no intention of petition-ing for custody. They aren't real eager to give me the time of day. I never even knew Carrie's mother. For all intents and purposes, our mother didn't raise either one of us. All I have going for me is half a set of genes. My lawyer's on it, but it could be weeks—months—before this is sorted out. Carrie could be adopted by then. Which would be fine, great for her, but then I'd have lost my chance. I don't want to take her. I won't hurt her. I just have to see her."

"I'm sorry, Mr. Kraynick, but…"

* * * * *

*Find out if Rick Kraynick will ever have a
chance to meet his niece.
Look for A DAUGHTER'S TRUST
by Tara Taylor Quinn,
available in September 2009.*

**We'll be spotlighting a different series
every month throughout 2009
to celebrate our 60th anniversary.**

**Look for Harlequin® Superromance®
in September!**

*Celebrate with
The Diamond Legacy
miniseries!*

Follow the stories of four cousins as they come to terms
with the complications of love and what it means to
be a family. Discover with them the sixty-year-old secret
that rocks not one but two families.

A DAUGHTER'S TRUST by *Tara Taylor Quinn*
September

FOR THE LOVE OF FAMILY by *Kathleen O'Brien*
October

LIKE FATHER, LIKE SON by *Karina Bliss*
November

A MOTHER'S SECRET by *Janice Kay Johnson*
December

Available wherever books are sold.

You're invited to join our Tell Harlequin Reader Panel!

By joining our new reader panel you will:

- Receive Harlequin® books—they are FREE and yours to keep with no obligation to purchase anything!
- Participate in fun online surveys
- Exchange opinions and ideas with women just like you
- Have a say in our new book ideas and help us publish the best in women's fiction

In addition, you will have a chance to win great prizes and receive special gifts! See Web site for details. Some conditions apply. Space is limited.

To join, visit us at

www.TellHarlequin.com.

REQUEST YOUR FREE BOOKS!

2 FREE NOVELS PLUS 2 FREE GIFTS!

HARLEQUIN®

INTRIGUE®

Breathtaking Romantic Suspense

YES! Please send me 2 FREE Harlequin Intrigue® novels and my 2 FREE gifts (gifts are worth about $10). After receiving them, if I don't wish to receive any more books, I can return the shipping statement marked "cancel." If I don't cancel, I will receive 6 brand-new novels every month and be billed just $4.24 per book in the U.S. or $4.99 per book in Canada. That's a savings of close to 15% off the cover price! It's quite a bargain! Shipping and handling is just 50¢ per book.* I understand that accepting the 2 free books and gifts places me under no obligation to buy anything. I can always return a shipment and cancel at any time. Even if I never buy another book from Harlequin, the two free books and gifts are mine to keep forever.

182 HDN EYTR 382 HDN EYT3

Name _____ (PLEASE PRINT) _____

Address _____ Apt. # _____

City _____ State/Prov. _____ Zip/Postal Code _____

Signature (if under 18, a parent or guardian must sign)

Mail to the **Harlequin Reader Service:**
IN U.S.A.: P.O. Box 1867, Buffalo, NY 14240-1867
IN CANADA: P.O. Box 609, Fort Erie, Ontario L2A 5X3

Not valid to current subscribers of Harlequin Intrigue books.

**Are you a current subscriber of Harlequin Intrigue books
and want to receive the larger-print edition?
Call 1-800-873-8635 today!**

* Terms and prices subject to change without notice. Prices do not include applicable taxes. Sales tax applicable in N.Y. Canadian residents will be charged applicable provincial taxes and GST. Offer not valid in Quebec. This offer is limited to one order per household. All orders subject to approval. Credit or debit balances in a customer's account(s) may be offset by any other outstanding balance owed by or to the customer. Please allow 4 to 6 weeks for delivery. Offer available while quantities last.

Your Privacy: Harlequin is committed to protecting your privacy. Our Privacy Policy is available online at www.eHarlequin.com or upon request from the Reader Service. From time to time we make our lists of customers available to reputable third parties who may have a product or service of interest to you. If you would prefer we not share your name and address, please check here. ☐

H109R

**Stay up-to-date
on all your romance
reading news!**

The Harlequin
Inside Romance
newsletter is a **FREE**
quarterly newsletter
highlighting
our upcoming
series releases
and promotions!

**Go to
eHarlequin.com/InsideRomance**
or e-mail us at
InsideRomance@Harlequin.com
to sign up to receive
your **FREE** newsletter today!

HARLEQUIN®

INTRIGUE®

COMING NEXT MONTH

Available September 8, 2009

#1155 SMOKIN' SIX-SHOOTER by B.J. Daniels
Whitehorse, Montana: The Corbetts
Although her new neighbor is all cowboy, she isn't looking for love—she wants answers to an unsolved murder. But when she digs too deep and invites the attention of a killer, her cowboy may be all that stands between her and a certain death.

#1156 AN UNEXPECTED CLUE by Elle James
Kenner County Crime Unit
When his cover is blown, the undercover FBI agent fears for the life of his wife and the child she carries. Although she no longer trusts him, he'll do whatever he has to do to save her and win back her love.

#1157 HIS SECRET LIFE by Debra Webb
Colby Agency: Elite Reconnaissance Division
Her mission is to find a hero who doesn't want to be found, but this Colby Agency P.I. always gets her man. She just doesn't count on the danger surrounding her target...or her irresistible attraction to him.

#1158 HIS BEST FRIEND'S BABY by Mallory Kane
Black Hills Brotherhood
When his best friend's baby is kidnapped, the rugged survival expert is on call to help rescue her child. As they follow the kidnapper's trail up a remote mountain, they must battle the elements and an undeniable passion.

#1159 PEEK-A-BOO PROTECTOR by Rita Herron
Seeing Double
The sheriff admires the work of the child advocate, but her latest charge, an abandoned baby, is the target of merciless kidnappers. Her life is on the line, and he's discovering that protecting her may be more than just a job....

#1160 COVERT COOTCHIE-COOTCHIE-COO
by Ann Voss Peterson
Seeing Double
Someone wants to harm the baby boy left aboard his ship, and the captain hires a tenacious P.I. to get some answers. As they work together to keep the child safe, startling truths are not the only things they uncover....

HICNMBPA0809